# EDUCATING DR. MAYFIELD

BOOK THREE

REBECCA HEFLIN

# ACKNOWLEDGMENTS

I can't believe this is my eighth book! From my first published book in 2011 to my eighth published book in 2017, I have had the support of my husband, my family, and my friends. They say writing is a solitary effort, but there are always those standing in the background, celebrating your achievements, holding your hand when you stumble, and brainstorming with you through the plotting snags. I dedicate this, and all my books to you. I thank you all from the bottom of my heart.

# QUOTE

"A loving heart is the beginning of all knowledge."
~ Thomas Carlyle

**1**

————

Green was not her best color.

Seated at a table in Sterling's one and only pub, Delaney Driscoll stared glumly across the table at her two best friends as they chattered about their upcoming weddings like two teenagers hopped-up on one-too-many energy drinks.

McGinty's Pub often played host to life's happiest and saddest events. It was where birthdays were toasted, engagements were announced, Sterling Bobcats wins were celebrated, and lives were remembered. It was only fitting that weddings should be planned there too.

Taking a swipe at the salt rimming her margarita, she stuck her finger in her mouth with a pout. She really needed to get over herself. Of course, she was ecstatic that her two best friends had found the loves of their lives. But, *come on.* Was it too much to ask that she find hers too?

"So, what do you think? Delaney? Earth to Delaney!" Sam snapped her fingers in front of her friend's face.

"Where were you?" Shelby asked, with a quizzical look.

"Oh. Sorry." She sighed then stuffed a fried pickle in her mouth.

Sam and Shelby exchanged glances.

"No, *we're* sorry. All this talk about our weddings must be boring you to tears," Sam said, a soft, understanding smile on her could've-been-a-model face.

Dr. Samantha Love, a psychology professor in the same college as Shelby and Delaney, had hit the news last year with a discovery the press called 'the love test'—a blood test that determined a couple's compatibility. One of the largest online dating services in the U.S. now offered the test as part of their premium package. And said 'love test' had found Sam's match in one Ethan Quinn, hunky literature professor and dean of their college. Now their wedding was just two months away—in April.

A whiz kid at statistics, Dr. Shelby Wentworth was a mathematics professor, first at Stanford, and then for a short stint at Sterling, before she became the Director of Sports Analytics for Sterling's athletics department. She and Sterling's head football coach, Nash Taylor, got engaged—on the football field, no less—after Sterling won its first NCAA Division I Football Bowl Subdivision Championship, thanks in part to Shelby's mad number-crunching skills. It was one of the most romantic proposals she and probably a million football fans had ever seen, thanks to an eagle-eyed cameraman who captured the moment, much to Nash and Shelby's chagrin.

Their wedding was coming up in June.

To make matters worse in the single department, Shelby, who had been Delaney's neighbor, moved out to Nash's farmhouse.

"Of course I'm not bored. I'm thrilled over both your

weddings, it's just I have a lot on my mind." Like being the loving, supportive, not-jealous friend she should be . . . among other things. She absently stirred her drink with a finger.

Shelby reached over and squeezed Delaney's free hand. "Tell me about your curriculum submission. Have you heard anything yet?"

"No. It's with the curriculum committee. Ethan thinks there shouldn't be any issues since I've done such a thorough job of incorporating existing courses, adding the few it needs, and because it's a timely major."

Delaney had been dreaming of creating a new major in her program—Bachelor of Fine Arts in Romantic Fiction and Literature—and now her packet was completed and in the hands of the university's curriculum committee. She'd been working on it, in between teaching and conducting scholarly research, for months. She wanted Sterling University to offer this new degree program in the course catalog that would come out next spring. A couple of the course additions were already on the fall class schedule.

"Well, when the decision comes down from on high, we'll have to celebrate." Sam held up her martini glass in salute, and Shelby followed suit with her own margarita.

Delaney played along and lifted her glass. "To writing—and teaching—romantic fiction."

They clinked glasses then took sips of their drinks. This being her second margarita, Delaney was beginning to feel the effects. Maybe she should stop there.

*Nah.* She'd walked the five blocks here, anyway.

The door to McGinty's opened and in walked—*hel-lo*—Mr. Tall, Dark, and Brooding. She sat up a little bit straighter.

She'd always been attracted to the Mr. Darcys of the world. The dark, forbidden men. The ones who so clearly needed the love of a good woman but didn't know it.

And this one fit the bill. Hair neatly cropped, the color of the mink stole her mom used to wear (before she went vegan), a strong chin with just a hint of stubble, and a body —clearly no stranger to the gym—that filled out the navy sweater he wore. Gray slacks. Conservative. And expensive, if she had to guess.

He walked over to the corner of the bar, away from the group huddled there watching NASCAR on the TV, and pulled up a barstool. Hugh McGinty, the pub's owner, approached and took his drink order. Scotch, neat. Shuddering, she wondered how anyone drank that, especially when good tequila was at hand.

She wondered if he was meeting someone. A woman, perhaps? Or a friend? She'd never seen him before, and with a population of sixteen thousand, including the students, it was rare to see someone in Sterling you didn't at least recognize. Was he new in town? Just visiting?

A comment from Shelby momentarily diverted her attention from Mr. TB&D to sigh over a picture of Shelby's wedding dress. A simple sleeveless, bateau-neck gown in white silk with three wide pleats across the front and a chapel-length train in the back. *Perfect.* "Oh, Shelby! It's lovely." Her enthusiasm returned. "When are we going to Atlanta to try it on?" The town of Sterling offered little in the way of wedding boutiques.

"Next weekend, if that's good for everyone. With the wedding only four months away, I've got to order it ASAP."

"That will be perfect. I can schedule my final fitting." Sam said as she checked her phone.

Delaney didn't bother checking her calendar. God knew

her weekends were free. Her weeknights, too, for that matter. "Works for me."

"Great! The guys will meet us for dinner later." Shelby entered the plans into her calendar.

*Super.* She'd be the fifth wheel. Again.

Delaney glanced back at the bar where Mr. TD&B sat. He had his drink in one hand, a magazine in the other. *Hmm.* Maybe he wasn't meeting anyone. Never one to pass up an opportunity, she chugged the rest of her drink. "Oh, look at that. I need another drink. Anyone else?"

Shelby and Delaney looked up from the bridal magazine they were studying.

"No, I'm good."

"Me too."

Delaney got up, maybe a tad too fast, given how the room spun. "Okey-dokey. I'll be back." Moistening her lips with a swipe of her tongue, she tossed her hair over her shoulder and made her way to the bar and the open spot next to him.

Signaling Hugh with her empty glass, she perched on the edge of the barstool, took a deep breath, turned her gaze on him, and stuck out her hand. "Hi, I'm Delaney Driscoll. You must be new in town." Although a bit tipsy, she thought she'd pulled that off with a dash of aplomb.

He shifted to look at her, put his magazine down, and held out his hand, albeit reluctantly. "Devon Mayfield." Distant. No smile.

But when his big warm hand wrapped around hers, she shivered. "Nice to meet you, Devon." *And you smell delish.*

"What was that?"

"What?" *Oh crap, did I just say that out loud?* Heat flooded her face. "Oh, I said, McGinty's food is delish."

He greeted her comeback with a muttered, "Good to know."

Hugh handed her another margarita. "I see you've met our Delaney here." He reached across and patted her on the cheek. "She's a good one, that's for sure."

The warmth of a blush crept into Delaney face at Hugh's words. Such a gem, that man.

Hugh continued, "You didn't have to come to the bar to order another drink. Why didn't you just signal Gabby? She would've taken your order."

"Pfft," Delaney said, with a wave of her hand. "I didn't want to bother Gabby. She's so busy." They all gazed in Gabby's direction, where she leaned against the register thumbing her phone.

*Or not.*

"Okay. Well. Thanks for the drink, Hugh," indicating—nicely, of course—that he should buzz off. Carefully lifting the full glass to her lips, she took a sip then turned back to Devon. "If you'd like, you can join my friends and me. We're just hanging out, talking about weddings." She winced. Nothing like wedding talk to entice a guy into joining you.

"Thanks, but I'm good here." He picked up his magazine as the now-busy Gabby brought him his dinner—McGinty's specialty—lamb stew.

Since he'd basically dismissed her, she said, "Alrighty, then. See ya 'round, *Devon.*"

*What a snob.*

She grinned.

*Just like Mr. Darcy.*

DEVON SHOOK his head as he watched one Delaney Driscoll weave her way back to her friends. Clearly, she'd already had one too many margaritas.

She dropped into the booth with an undignified plop and leaned over the table to whisper something to the women across from her.

They all lifted their gazes in his direction. Raising a brow along with his glass of scotch, he saluted them. Only one had the nerve to hold eye contact—the pretty blonde. She hefted her martini glass in return.

Feeling oddly self-conscious, he broke eye contact and turned his attention to the tantalizing aroma of lamb stew and the article in the latest issue of the *American Journal of Business Education*.

As the new dean for Sterling's College of Business, he'd had a mandate: to make the college one of the top ten business schools in the country by the end of his third year as dean. A tall order, but one he believed he could fulfill. They only had to move up six slots in the rankings. An achievable goal with the right leadership and teamwork.

Nestled in the hills of Northeast Georgia, the town of Sterling owed its existence to two things: granite and knowledge. Granite, because Sterling held some of the richest granite quarries in the world—if it was made of granite, it probably came from Sterling—and knowledge, because Sterling University—one of the Southern Ivy League schools, a.k.a. The Magnolia League—educated almost ten thousand students inside its hallowed halls and sent them out into the world to share that knowledge.

While researching the job offer, Devon learned that the university was founded in 1835 by wealthy granite quarry magnate and town founder Samuel Sterling. The university's arts department even offered classes in granite-carving, and of course its geology program was one of the country's best. Sterling had endowed the university with one million dollars and three hundred and fifty acres of land adjacent to the family home.

When the last of the Sterling line, Victoria Eliza Sterling-Pickard, died in 1974, she left the family home to the university for use as its main administration building, aptly named Sterling Hall.

Devon quickly discovered that if you lived in or around Sterling, you most likely either worked for the university or for one of the many granite quarries or monument-makers.

An outburst of giggles drew his attention back to the booth of three women. Attractive women at that, each in their own way. The cool blonde was polished and sophisticated—classic. The petite one with light brown hair was fresh-faced and casual—the quintessential girl next door.

But Delaney, with her golden-blond hair and curvy figure, was a bombshell. And when he'd responded to her introduction, he'd been momentarily stunned by the most arresting blue eyes he'd ever seen. No. Not just blue . . . sapphire.

He had to admit, she'd smelled nice too. Something sweet but light, like orange blossoms.

But he'd also been unnerved by that direct gaze. She'd looked at him like she could see right through his armor to the parts underneath that had been found lacking by those who should've loved him unconditionally.

The subject of his assessment snorted then burst into another fit of giggles.

Clearly ditzy, though. Not his type at all.

He liked smart, sophisticated women, with excellent manners and polished social skills. Someone with goals of her own and the determination and drive to meet them.

Delaney slapped the table with her hands, laughing—no, *guffawing*—at something her companions said.

*Definitely* not his type.

He needed a woman and a partner, someone who would support him and who would be an asset to him in the pursuit of his goals while she also pursued her own. Someone who would make a respectable first lady to the president of an Ivy League university. Preferably someone in academe.

And to that end, he ignored the women and returned to his journal article on business and computer science degrees and job satisfaction in a vain attempt to turn a deaf ear to the still-giggling threesome.

DEVON HAD JUST PAID his tab and was preparing to leave when two other men walked into McGinty's. He recognized one from the dean's meeting last week. Ethan Quinn, dean of the College of Arts and Sciences. He didn't know the other man, although he looked familiar.

After scanning the dining area, they made their way to the table of three women. The blonde rose from her seat, and Ethan gathered her into his arms, kissing her on the mouth. Well, that ended that. He'd thought to introduce himself to her at some point, strike up a conversation and see if she was interested. Clearly not.

The other man took the Girl Next Door's hand and pulled her in for a kiss as well, while the Blonde Bombshell looked on, a touch of envy evident in the pout.

Not only flighty, but an egg-timer on the final countdown. All the more reason to steer clear.

Devon picked up his magazine and headed for the door.

"Oh, Devon."

He turned to see Ethan waving him over. *Great.*

"Devon, let me introduce you," Ethan said as he stood. "Devon is the new dean of the College of Business. And this is Nash Taylor, head football coach."

*Ah.* That explains why he'd looked familiar. "You used to play for the Broncos." Devon stuck out his hand.

Nash nodded and shook it. "Nice to meet you. This is my fiancée, Shelby Wentworth," he said, as he gestured to the Girl Next Door.

"And, this is *my* fiancée, Samantha Love," Ethan continued, taking the Polished Sophisticate's hand.

*Fiancée?* Definitely off limits then. "Pleasure." So, that's the lay of the land. The weddings they were talking about were Bombshell's friends'.

"Oh, and I believe you two met—this is Delaney Driscoll," Samantha interjected.

"Yes. We met."

Delaney narrowed her eyes at him like she had his number.

"Settling in to life in Sterling?" Ethan asked.

"Yes. I'm closing on my townhouse in Georgetown Square next week."

"I used to live in Georgetown Square," Samantha said. "You'll love it. Very quiet. Nice neighbors."

"Good to know."

"We're putting together a little three-on-three basketball game tomorrow, and we just lost our third," Ethan said. "Care to join?"

"Sure. What time and where?" Devon asked. He needed the exercise, and a little competition couldn't hurt.

"Four o'clock at the Granite Park courts."

"I'll see you then. Nice meeting everyone." As he moved

to the door, he could feel a pair of eyes boring into his back. And he'd just bet those eyes were the color of the Mediterranean Sea.

His shoulder blades itched with the thought that she could see far more than he wanted her to.

## 2

The following Saturday, as Taylor Swift sang at full volume about never getting back together, Delaney put the finishing touches on her appearance. Not that there was anyone who would notice.

Grabbing her purse, she walked into the living room just as the doorbell rang. Swinging open the door, she invited Shelby in.

"You ready?" Shelby asked. But before Delaney could answer, Shelby continued, "Oh no. You're listening to Taylor Swift, and that can only mean one thing."

Shelby followed her into the kitchen. "Mason and I broke up. Again." Story of her life. She couldn't make a man stick if she stripped naked and rubbed herself in Elmer's Glue.

"I thought you broke up two weeks ago."

"We did." She put her coffee mug in the dishwasher. "But we got back together on Tuesday. And broke up again yesterday. Thus," she waved her hand in the direction of her iPod docking station, "the song."

Shelby shook her head. "Sounds like you should take Taylor's advice this time. You feel up to Atlanta?"

"Of course!" She put on a smile. "Are you kidding me? I wouldn't miss it." *What was a little salt in the wound when it came to her best friends' weddings?*

"Great. Sam's waiting in the car. The guys will join us later for dinner."

"Perfect." Just what she wanted—to be the tag along at a couples' dinner. A soon-to-be-*married* couples' dinner.

As they headed for the door, Shelby said, "I thought you didn't really like Mason because he stared at his own reflection too much."

"Beggars can't be choosers." Delaney locked up and tossed her keys into her purse with disgust.

Before she could take a step toward the car, Shelby took her by the shoulders and looked her in the eye. "You're not a beggar. Far from it. And you *should* be choosy. You deserve the best. Not some guy who's in love with his own appearance. It will happen. I know it."

"Yeah, well, care to run some numbers for me? Do the stats show it will happen before my eggs expire?"

"Listen to me. It will happen when you least expect it. Stop trying so hard. Focus on your career goals, the new major you've created, and the rest will fall into place."

"From your mouth to Cupid's ears," Delaney muttered, as she followed Shelby to Sam's waiting car.

THE PROVOST HAD APPOINTED Devon to the university's curriculum committee, contending the experience would provide useful information in pursuing his own college's goals. Since he wouldn't assume any teaching responsibilities until fall, he had the time to commit to the workload the committee position entailed.

So, bright and early Monday morning, he picked up the week's committee meeting packets that had been dropped off with his assistant and thumbed through them. An interesting mix of new courses, new majors, some new syllabi, and a few certificate programs.

To his mind, a college course or major needed to prepare a student for meaningful work in his or her chosen field. Impart skills that would be appealing to a potential employer. Some life skills courses were useful too, like etiquette, communication, and personal finances.

He frowned upon the so-called 'basket-weaving courses' that some students liked to take for an easy A. What good would Zombies in Popular Culture or The Science of Harry Potter do for someone seeking lucrative employment? Students needed structure and real-world experiences in their education. Not touchy-feely pop culture nonsense.

His own education had been very structured, almost militaristic in its formality. He'd attended an exclusive boarding school in Connecticut for the entirety of his primary and secondary education, and while it wasn't a military academy, his days were structured to the minute. From the time he'd wake up at 6 a.m. to lights out at 10 p.m., his day had been filled with everything from classes to study hall and physical education, as well as life skills training like financial management and budgeting, time management, and etiquette.

By the age of fifteen, he knew which fork to use with fish, how to balance a checkbook, budget for savings, and make informed financial decisions. Not that he had much money for any of those things. But what little he'd had, he'd handled judiciously.

Abandoned by his mother who'd left him with a wealthy man, presumably his father, who'd had little to nothing to do with Devon, he'd learned quickly to stand on his own two feet.

So, when it came time to go to college, Devon chose not to seek assistance from the man. Rather, he applied to the top business schools in the country, and was accepted into many, but selected Harvard when they offered him a full scholarship. He'd worked for a short time in a bookstore to cover his living and other expenses.

Money no longer an issue—he'd solved that problem when he'd created and sold two start-ups before he graduated—he could now do whatever he wanted for a living. And what he wanted was to impart his knowledge to the world's future business leaders and apply the business strategies he'd learned to institutions of higher education.

And while money was no longer his goal, respect was. Even if love wasn't in the cards for him, he would be respected. To that end, he had his sights set on moving up the ranks to provost and eventually president of a prestigious university, with a proper wife by his side.

Flipping to the last packet in the stack, he caught the name Delaney Driscoll, Ph.D.

He sat up. The Blonde Bombshell was a faculty member? Setting the packet aside, he searched for her profile on the university's website. It was her alright. The photo was unmistakably Delaney. Those eyes, that hair. And the smile. Nothing fake in that. It showed in her eyes.

He wondered what her life had been like to make her so open and . . . engaging.

Scrolling down, he read her *vitae*—Born and raised in Kansas. Attended Middlebury College in Vermont, earning her bachelor's degree in English lit, before heading off to the

University of Denver for both her master's and Ph.D. in English and creative writing respectively. Returned to Middlebury College following graduation to teach. A few years ago, she took a position at Sterling in their newly formed creative writing program.

Creative writing. Why didn't that surprise him?

Not that there was anything wrong with that. He enjoyed a good novel now and again. John le Carré and Tom Clancy came to mind.

But when he scrolled down to the list of courses Delaney taught, he rolled his eyes. Girl Power and The Young Adult Novel. "What the hell is that?" he muttered. The course readings included the *Twilight* novels and *The Hunger Games* series. "This is what she teaches?"

The next course on the list was Literature and Women's Sexuality. *Good Lord.* He skimmed the readings covered in the course: *Madame Bovary, Tess of the d'Urbervilles, Lady Chatterley's Lover, The Kadin,* whatever that was, and . . . "*Fifty Shades of Grey*?!"

"Did you say something, Dr. Mayfield?" Rachel, his assistant, popped her head in the doorway.

He cleared his throat in embarrassment. "No, Rachel. Thanks."

He scrolled back up to the photo of Miss Sexpot, and a vivid recollection of her curves and her scent accosted him. Maybe . . . "No." Not going there. He needed a wife, not a fling.

Even so, curiosity got the better of him and he opened the packet to see what she'd submitted. A new major in the creative writing program—BFA in Romantic Fiction and Literature. Gazing skyward, he muttered. "Figures."

～

THE UNIVERSITY'S curriculum committee had been at the March meeting's agenda for over an hour, voting to approve various new courses, a few certificates, and one new major. They'd also voted to deny a new course in engineering called The Science of Star Trek.

That one deserved a dose of scorn.

Devon looked at the next item on the agenda. Dr. Driscoll's new major. He glanced over at her, seated in a chair along the wall, wearing a suit that on most women would be modest, but on her, it all but screamed sexy secretary.

Dr. Morton Gregors, the committee chair, introduced the proposal, bringing Devon's attention back to the table.

A derisive snort came from the curmudgeonly Dr. Gordon. Out of the corner of his eye, he saw Delaney sit up, clearly affronted.

"Aren't those the books with long-haired shirtless men and busty women my cheatin' ex-wife was always readin'?" Dr. Gordon asked, a scowl on his florid face. His heavy accent belied a sharp mind, albeit with a sharp tongue to match.

"You're thinking of romance novels from the eighties," Angela Burton, chemistry professor, said waving her hand dismissively. "They've changed in the three decades since."

Dr. Gordon greeted her remark with a raised eyebrow. "I guess you *read* those rags?"

"I do, and I'm not ashamed to admit it," she said, with an indignant sniff.

"I think it's worthy of consideration," Dr. Adams, history professor, said. "We've certainly approved new majors for other degrees that may have been less marketable. Take the major we approved last year in the College of Journalism—Bachelor of Arts in Culinary Criticism."

Devon's head popped up from the notes he'd been reading. *Seriously?*

"At least there's a market for romantic fiction," Dr. Adams continued.

A few nods followed.

"It's absurd." Dr. Gordon slapped the table.

Dr. Gregors held up a hand. "If we could dispense with the judgments regarding one's choice of literature–"

"Hmph. Literature," Dr. Gordon muttered, receiving a glare from Dr. Burton.

"As I was saying, the issue is not whether romantic fiction is worthy of a read. It's whether this would be a legitimate program of study to be added to our curriculum. Will the granting of the degree prepare our students to enter a lucrative job market, are there enough students interested in such a degree, and is this is a defensible use of our resources?"

"That's simple enough," Dr. Gordon chimed in. "It's a total waste of resources." He folded his arms across his chest.

Dr. Burton bristled at the opinion. "Dr. Gordon, are you deeming romantic fiction unworthy because it is a female-dominated industry? Literature written *by* women *for* women?"

"There's that word again. *Literature.* I hardly think romance novels are worthy of being included in that category with the likes of Hemingway, Fitzgerald, and Twain."

Dr. Burton crossed her arms over her chest, echoing his body language. "Funny, no women included in that lineup."

Dr. Gordon answered with a contemptuous hand wave, a scowl on his face.

Devon shifted uncomfortably in his seat. While he didn't agree that the degree was a valuable addition to the Sterling student catalog, he didn't approve of Dr. Gordon's rude and clearly biased tone.

If the responses to Dr. Gregors' key questions were 'yes,' then regardless of what one thought of the subject matter, it deserved the committee's consideration.

But he happened to think the answers to the questions were 'no.'

He cleared his throat, drawing the interest of the other committee members. "I realize this is my first committee meeting, and while I may not agree with some of Dr. Gordon's comments, I do agree that this proposed new major is not viable, strictly for practical reasons."

Now that he had their full attention, and the bickering had ceased, he continued, not risking a glance in Dr. Driscoll's direction. "Rising tides lift all boats. As you know, one of the criteria used to rank colleges and universities is their career placement."

"For those of you in colleges and programs—like the College of Business—that are part of the president's initiative to rise in the rankings, having a glut of dead-end majors ultimately impacts you, even if those degree programs are not in your college." He tapped the proposal packet with this finger. "This appears to be one of those dead-end programs."

Dr. Applebaum, from the College of Arts and Sciences, chimed in. "We have degrees in arts programs which might fall into the same so-called 'dead-end' category. Our graduates won't necessarily be *hired*, although certainly some will seek jobs in museums and galleries, but many will create art for sale. Are you saying our BFAs in sculpture or painting are dead-end degrees?"

Devon glanced around the table then looked back at Dr. Applebaum. "At least, if the graduate doesn't make it in the art world, he or she can teach sculpture or painting, or like you said, seek employment elsewhere in the art world. But who would hire someone with a BFA in Romantic Fiction to teach literature or work in a library?"

There were comments around the table, some nods of agreement, but also some skepticism.

"Sterling's motto is 'Preparing our students for today, tomorrow, and beyond,'" Devon continued. "It is the university's responsibility to give our students the tools they need to succeed in an increasingly complicated world. I hardly think Reading the Romance Novel is one of those tools."

An indignant sniff came from Delaney's direction.

"I can't help but believe that there is some degree of discrimination here," Dr. Burton stated.

"Perhaps, on the part of some of us," Dr. Gregors agreed, as he leveled a glare at Dr. Gordon. "But, be that as it may, Dr. Mayfield is right. There is not enough evidence here," he held up the proposal, "to convince me that this is a viable degree."

"Agree," Dr. Applebaum said.

"I make a motion to deny the proposal," Dr. Gordon said, raising his hand.

Devon sighed, disgusted to be the one to second the man's motion. "And I second the motion."

"All those in favor of denying Dr. Driscoll's proposal for a BFA in Romantic Fiction and Literature say *aye*."

Devon scanned the votes. All ayes except Dr. Burton.

"Those opposed."

Dr. Burton raised her hand, a frown on her face.

"Motion carries. This meeting is adjourned."

3

<hr>

Delaney selected a pool cue from the rack and chalked the tip.

Hanging with her girls on a Thursday night at McGinty's was the highlight of what was an otherwise crap-tastic week. She intended to let off some steam and forget all about Devon Mayfield and the committee's narrow-minded view of education curriculum. With the exception of Angela Burton. Not to mention, Devon's apparent ability to turn otherwise open-minded professors on the curriculum committee, like Dr. Applebaum and Dr. Gregors, into his supporters.

"I mean, *come on*, the curriculum committee approved a certificate program in online video gaming just last year," she continued her complaints, as she picked up her margarita.

"I thought the point of tonight's activities was to take your mind off the subject." Shelby gathered up the balls and rolled them to the other end of the table. "What would Taylor Swift say?"

"Haters gonna hate." Delaney walked to the opposite end of the table.

"And what else would she say?" Sam added.

"Shake it off," Delaney muttered.

"Exactly," Shelby said, her voice emphatic.

"You're right. I won't bring it up again." Delaney placed the cue ball on the dot and bent over to break the balls. She popped up again. "It's just, without him rallying the troops, I think my proposal would have had more supporters. Dr. Applebaum could have been swayed, as well as Dr. Gregors."

Other than the crotchety old Dr. Gordon, there were plenty of head nods around that table. "You should have heard Devon calling the degree a dead-end." She threw up her free hand. "What does he know?"

Sam rolled her eyes and heaved a sigh. "You're right. But the question is: What are you going to do about it?"

"I don't know yet. But . . . something." This time she took her shot and sank a stripe in the far left corner. She missed her next shot—a bank—which was a tad over her skill level anyway.

Shelby stalked the table searching for an open shot. "I think you need to look at it from his perspective." Bending over the table, she cued up. "Four ball, side pocket."

"Shel, we don't need to call the pockets," Sam reminded her, leaning on her pool cue.

Shelby shrugged as the ball rolled in. "Habit."

Delaney put her free hand on her hip. "What do you mean, I need to see it from his perspective?"

"Now, don't get your knickers in a twist." Shelby crossed to the other side of the table. "He's a business professor—a Harvard MBA, Wharton, Ph.D.—you need to make your case with facts and figures. Data."

"Ugh." Delaney threw her head back. "You know me and numbers." She couldn't figure out her restaurant tab, much less run numbers on the romantic fiction industry.

"Yes, I do." Shelby sank two balls in one shot, both solid. "But you happen to have a friend who's very good with numbers."

"And running the pool table," Sam muttered.

"Sometimes I get lucky," Shelby said with a grin. "Anyway, I could help you." She stood, pool stick resting on the ground, and gazed across the table at Delaney.

Yeah. Shelby was a genius when it came to numbers. She could figure out a five-person restaurant tab, with tip, in her head. For that reason alone, Delaney worshipped her. Then there was the FBS Championship title that Sterling won earlier this year, thanks in part to Shelby's magic with numbers. "You'd do that?"

"Of course. What are friends for?"

"Ladies."

Delaney turned to see Nash and Ethan strolling over to the billiard tables looking handsome and happy.

Nash wrapped an arm around Shelby's waist and kissed her. Ethan followed suit with Sam.

And there Delaney stood, odd woman out. Again.

"Hi, guys." She nodded.

"We don't want to interrupt ladies' night out," Ethan said. "Just wanted to say hi."

"Yeah, we're meeting Devon for dinner," Nash explained.

Delaney shoved Nash, who didn't budge an inch. "How can you hang out with that jerk?"

Nash chuckled. "Jerk? I admit he's a bit stiff, but he's a nice enough guy."

"Apparently, Devon had a hand in throwing a monkeywrench into approving Delaney's proposed new major," Ethan supplied.

"Oh. Well, I'm sure you'll convince him otherwise." Nash bent his six-foot-four-inch frame to look her in the eye. "You can be very persuasive when you want something badly enough."

Delaney knew he was remembering her role in convincing him to fly down to Miami to apologize to Shelby when everything went FUBAR.

He straightened and, taking Shelby's hand, said, "See you later. Try not to run the table on these two."

Sam snorted. "Too late for that."

WHEN DEVON ENTERED MCGINTY'S, he spotted Nash and Ethan already at a booth. The place was busy for a Thursday night, but what did he expect? A pub in a college town was bound to be a popular hangout.

He nodded to a grad student from his college and took a seat next to Nash. He appreciated Nash and Ethan's attempts at befriending him. He didn't crave the company of others very often, but it had been nice to have a couple of guys to grab a meal with or go a few rounds on the basketball court.

Even so, he didn't expect to be best man at their weddings or anything.

After greeting the guys, he picked up his menu. He'd yet to have one of McGinty's juicy burgers, but he'd worked up an appetite on his run this afternoon.

The waitress took their drink order. The guys ordered a craft beer. When it was his turn, he said, "You know what, that sounds good. I'll have the same." Burger and beer. Not since his college days.

"You settled in?" Nash asked.

"Yes. I moved into the townhouse, learning my way around, and getting the lay of the land in the college as well."

"Well, if you need any help moving furniture or anything, we're happy to help."

"Thanks, but I think I'm good." But he appreciated the offer just the same.

A guffaw of laughter reached him. A guffaw he recognized immediately. Delaney was here?

"The women are back by the billiard tables." Ethan thumbed behind him, as if reading his mind. "Ladies night."

Shelby crossed his line of sight, but he didn't see Delaney. Probably for the best. Needless to say, she wasn't too happy with him or the committee right now.

Nash and Ethan eyed each other.

"What?" Devon prompted.

Ethan shook his head. "Not really my place."

"I see." Devon moved the salt-shaker out of the way then propped his elbows on the table. "Delaney told you about the committee's review."

"Yeah." Ethan lifted his hands. "But I've already done my part and approved it at the college level. I'm not going to interfere with the committee's consideration."

Devon nodded. "I know Delaney is your friend, so I appreciate that."

The waitress brought their drinks and took their dinner orders.

That frosty beer looked delicious. Devon picked up the mug and took a long, satisfying pull. At that moment, Delaney stepped into his line of vision and bent over the pool table, her curvaceous ass on full display in a pair of snug blue jeans.

And the beer went down the wrong pipe.

Coughing like he'd swallowed Lake Michigan, his eyes watered and he set the mug on the table, trying in vain to draw in a breath.

Nash pounded him on the back. "You okay?"

Devon couldn't respond as his throat continued to spasm. He picked up the napkin to wipe the tears from his eyes. *Jesus!*

Besides enduring the physical discomfort, he now suffered the humiliation of having nearby patrons gawking at him. When he cleared the tears from his eyes, he saw Delaney, one hand on her hip, pool cue in the other, glaring at him.

*Perfect. Just perfect.*

Why didn't he just charge admittance to the sideshow he'd become?

He threw his napkin on the table and rose. Still unable to utter a word, he raised his index finger, indicating to Nash and Ethan that he'd be right back, and then he bolted to the men's room, where he hoped he could regain control of both his spasming epiglottis and his composure.

DELANEY FOLLOWED Devon's progress to the back of the pub where the restrooms were. Maybe he choked on his own arrogance.

She winced at her uncharitable thought. He appeared to be in distress, and as much as she hated him, she hoped he'd be okay.

Sort of.

"Delaney? You going to take your shot?" Sam asked.

"Yeah." She bent over the table, lined up with the cue ball, then sighed and stood up. "Be right back."

"Don't do it, girlfriend," Sam warned.

"Do what?" Delaney asked, all innocence. "I've got to pee."

"Uh huh. I'm taking your turn," Shelby threatened.

"Fine. Maybe you'll actually make the shot."

Devon came out of the men's room, looking all emotionally unavailable, and she really wanted to rattle his chain. He stopped short when he saw her there. "Come to see if I'd choked to death?"

"No, not to *death*." She flashed him a cheeky grin. "But I wouldn't mind, say, a mild coma." She crossed her arms.

"Is there anything else you wanted besides gloating over my discomfort?"

"As a matter of fact, I wanted to tell you this isn't over. I'll be resubmitting my proposal."

"Fine. We'll review it per the committee's guidelines."

"Good. And just so you know, I won't give up without a fight."

"Clearly. But you should consider addressing some of the committee's concerns."

Struck by his constructive comment, she narrowed her eyes at him. "The committee's or yours?"

"Both. Goodnight, Dr. Driscoll. Now, if you don't mind, I'd like to see if my dinner has been served yet."

"Don't mind a bit." Delaney stepped aside, and Devon strode past her, leaving a spicy, masculine scent behind. And damn if it didn't make her knees go weak.

*Damn knees.*

## 4

---

fter spending most of his life in the Northeast, March in Sterling was a welcome change. The temperatures were still cool, but the warm sun on his back hinted at the promise of spring as Devon walked across campus, a hot coffee on his mind.

A sidewalk wound its way through a particularly picturesque section of campus, where moss-covered oaks likely offered a welcome respite from the hot sun in summer. The azaleas and dogwoods showed signs of the flowers to come.

Students sat at picnic tables scattered beneath the trees. Others sat on the ground, computers in their laps, while still others used their backpacks as pillows and stretched out for afternoon naps in spots of sun.

Perhaps because he grew up on a school campus, he felt most at home on one now.

He arrived at his destination—Uncommon Grounds, the campus coffee shop. Rachel had offered to get a coffee for him, but he wanted the fresh air, and to see more of the campus.

He queued up at the end of the line, checking out the chalk menu above the counter.

The offerings had a decidedly Southern twist, including praline coffee, with brown sugar and vanilla cream; pecan hot chocolate topped with whipped cream, maple syrup, and chopped pecans; and something called Moonlight and Magnolias—roasted chicory-root coffee blended with cinnamon and vanilla cream and topped with a dollop of chocolate whipped cream.

In deference to his sweet tooth, he decided on the praline coffee, and stepped up to a tattoo-covered barista to give his order. As he waited for his coffee, he spotted Delaney at a table in the corner, her laptop open. Probably reading *Fifty Shades of Grey*. He snorted. But just as he was about to turn his back on her, she dropped her head into her hand.

Was she crying over the committee's decision? Was something wrong? Did she get bad news?

Not his problem, he reminded himself.

*Aw, hell.* Did she just wipe a tear from her cheek?

The barista didn't bother calling his name, since he was still standing at the counter. He took his coffee and told himself to just keep walking out the door and back to Fisher Hall, which housed the College of Business. He had work piled on his desk that required his attention.

But somehow his feet took over and he found himself standing next to Delaney's table. She didn't seem to notice. Then she sniffed and lifted her head, startled by his presence.

"What?" she asked, a little defiant. She'd definitely been crying. "Come to criticize my proposal again? Didn't get in enough at the committee meeting?"

He cleared his throat. This is what he got when his feet

overruled his brain. "I couldn't help but notice you seemed upset."

She brushed another tear away. If there was one thing that broke through his thick skin, it was a woman crying.

He drew up a chair, without asking her permission. "Anything I can help you with?"

"No." Her chin lifted a hair.

He waited a moment to see if she was going to speak further. When she didn't, he decided it was best to leave her alone, and he started to rise.

"Eliot died." She sniffed again, as her eyes welled up.

*Good Lord!* Who was Eliot? A brother? A boyfriend? How to broach that subject? "I'm so sorry."

"I loved that cat!"

*Cat? Eliot was a cat?* "I'm sorry, did you say cat?"

"Yes," she blubbered. "T.S. Eliot."

He yanked a few napkins out of the dispenser on the table and handed them to her.

She blew her nose and wiped her eyes. "Thank you."

All this over a *cat*?

He'd never owned a pet. Never understood the purpose of sharing one's home with a furry creature that clawed up the furniture, pissed on the carpet, and shed all over everything.

He studied Delaney's face. Red-rimmed eyes, blotchy tear-streaked cheeks, runny nose. She shouldn't look the least bit attractive. Not many women would, under the circumstances, but for some reason she did. She looked . . . endearing.

"I've had Eliot since I was twelve."

*Twelve?* "I see." Even though he didn't. How old was Delaney? "And, how old was Eliot?"

"Seventeen."

*Seventeen!* That would make her twenty-nine. Six years younger than himself. The perfect age difference to his mind.

And why, exactly, should he care?

She sniffled. What should he say to comfort her? He had no experience with this sort of thing. "Well, sounds like he lived a long and happy life."

"Yes. He did." She dabbed at her eyes. "And I knew this day would come, but you're never ready, you know?" she asked, looking to him for confirmation of her feelings.

"I, uh, I know." Even though he really didn't.

"Did you have pets growing up?"

"No. Pets weren't allowed where I grew up."

"Oh. That's sad. And lonely." She gazed up at him with those big blue weepy eyes, and he almost regretted not having a pet.

"Have you, uh, provided for the animal's . . ." he continued, trying to choose his words carefully, "burial?" Perhaps he could call one of her friends for her, to help her with the arrangements. What does one do with a pet that has, er, well, croaked?

"My mother had him cremated."

"Already? When did he die?"

"Two days ago."

*Two days!* And she's still bawling about it? "And, your mother is here?"

"No. She's in Kansas."

He gave himself a mental headshake. "I don't understand." If the cat was here, how did her mother have him cremated in Kansas?

"Eliot lived with my mother because I couldn't have him in the university residence halls, and then I was moving, and then, well, then he was just too old to uproot and bring here."

"How long has it been since you've seen Eliot?" She's grieving a cat that didn't even live with her?

"Two years." She wiped her eyes with a napkin, leaving a streak of mascara behind. "And now I'm wracked with guilt. He died, without me there to hold him."

Annnd the weeping began anew.

He looked around, trying to figure out how to extricate himself from this . . . predicament.

"Is there someone I can call?"

"No. Thank you." She scrubbed her face again with the napkins, further streaking her makeup. "I'll be fine." She gave him a watery smile.

Maybe that was his cue to exit the scene. He nodded. "Do you have a mirror?"

"Yes, why?"

He pointed to his eyes, "You might want to, you know, clean up a bit."

"Oh. Yes." She laughed, and it was as if someone reached in and squeezed his heart. He'd made Delaney Driscoll smile through her tears.

"Well. I should go. I have to get back to work."

"Thanks for talking to me, Devon."

He nodded as he rose, coffee in hand, then hesitated. "You should know that it's nothing personal—my disapproval of your proposal, that is."

"Well, it feels personal, Devon." She gazed up at him with watery eyes. "Especially when the committee has already approved all the proposals that were submitted at the same time as mine. That feels personal. And when one of the reasons for denying the proposal was a blatant disdain for the subject matter. That feels pretty personal too."

Damn Dr. Gordon and his condescension. "The committee's decision is not personal," he reiterated. "*My* decision is not personal."

She rolled her eyes and snorted.

He simply nodded again, and with that high-tailed it out of there. Stepping outside, he took a deep breath. What a mess.

DELANEY BLEW HER NOSE AGAIN, as she watched Devon walk through the coffee shop door and out into the cool spring air. He was such a jerk. And then he did something nice. Like just now. Then he had to turn back into the jerk, as if 'nice Devon' had to have an expiration.

*It's nothing personal.* Easy for him to say. She'd put her blood, sweat, and tears into creating interesting, challenging, evocative courses for her students. And it was no different with the degree program she proposed.

She had been steadily submitting new courses to the curriculum committee in preparation for the new major. They'd approved them all. And now they balked at the major? What did they think she was doing when she submitted proposals like Reading the Romance Novel, Publishing Romantic Fiction, and the foundation courses, Writing the Romance Novel I and II?

Finding her compact, she opened it up to check out the damage. "Ugh." How humiliating. She looked like a psycho clown. After dipping a napkin in her glass of water, she dabbed at the streaks of mascara. Then she took the powder puff out and touched up her face with the powder. A swipe of lip gloss, and it would have to do. She had a class to teach in half an hour.

Gathering her laptop, notes, and purse, she packed them into her tote bag. She'd been researching the romantic fiction market, in preparation for her resubmission, when her computer wallpaper photo of Eliot had triggered another crying jag.

Devon Mayfield thought she was a flighty ditz. But she'd show him and the rest of the committee. With a little help from her number-crunching friend, Shelby. As Shelby and Sam pointed out, while she might be a liberal arts professor, she needed to argue her case in a language Devon would understand. She just needed Shelby to help her create those colorful pie charts and graphs. A skill totally foreign to her.

She'd discovered all kind of stats on the market. Stats that would impress a businessman like Devon. He thought writing romantic fiction was a dead-end career with no possibility of success. She'd show him.

In the end, she'd earn the curriculum committee's approval. With or without Devon's vote. And of course, that of crotchety old Dr. Gordon.

**5**

———

"So, I understand Sam is running another research study on her love test?" Nash asked, as he settled on the weight bench next to where Devon performed a set of arm curls.

Devon had run into Ethan and Nash in Granite Fitness during lunch, and they'd added him to their weight circuit.

Ethan wiped sweat from his face with a towel and stood ready to spot Nash as he bench-pressed. "Yeah. She's refining the assay to avoid the possibility of double matches like she had with me and a few other participants."

Devon listened to the conversation, unsure what they were talking about. "What sort of test is this?"

Ethan shook his head with a laugh. "Maybe a little background first, because it sounds rather clinical and impersonal. Let's see if I can get this right."

"Humans are often attracted to people who possess a particular set of genes called major histocompatibility complex, or MHC," he began. "MHC plays a critical role in the ability to fight viruses. Mates with dissimilar MHC genes produce healthier offspring with broad immune systems. It's an evolutionary thing, but Sam discovered its predictive value—like in whether couples will have long, happy relationships."

"Well," Ethan continued, as he took the barbell from Nash and set it in the stand. "Sam discovered a blood chemical, which she calls MHC-P1, that predicts MHC, and through her previous research, she's proven that couples whose MHC-P1 were on opposite ends of the spectrum, indicating their MHC genes were dissimilar, had longer, happier relationships—and healthier, more productive children."

Intrigued, Devon asked, "How did she prove this?"

"By taking blood samples, conducting interviews with, and administering compatibility questionnaires to, happily attached couples who have been together twenty years or more."

"Compatibility questionnaires like the ones online dating services use?" Devon set aside the dumbbell then took a gulp of water.

"Correct. She had a control group of some five thousand couples, married for at least twenty years. She gave them the questionnaire and took their blood. A high percentage of those who reported that they are happily married—or otherwise attached—showed strong chemical compatibility, similar to that of the questionnaires."

Nash prepared for another set of bench-presses, so Ethan paused in his explanation to spot him.

"She also had a cohort, to which both she and I belonged, of another five thousand single or divorced men and women who took the same questionnaire and blood test. She ran the tests against those individuals in the database, and when she found matches, she compared the chemical compatibility to the questionnaire compatibility. A statistically significant percentage of the time, when the blood chemistry inversely matched, the compatibility questionnaires matched as well."

"And you said the two of you were in the database. Were you a match?"

"Yes." Ethan guided the barbell to the stand again.

"But he also matched with another woman in town," Nash interjected as he rose from the weight bench.

Devon thought he saw Ethan shudder.

"So, what happened there?"

"Sam thinks that some people will have more than one match. After all, some people will have more than one successful relationship in their lives that ends through no fault of their own, like with the death of a partner. But later, they may find another partner with whom they spend the rest of their lives."

Interest piqued, Devon prompted Ethan. "And she's running this new study to refine the test?"

"Yeah. She's discovered a way to refine the levels of MHC-P1, but she needs to test the new assay against those individuals in the database whose results are from the original assay."

This could be the answer for him. Devon didn't have time to play the dating game. And the thought of going on an online dating site gave him hives. But a blood test? Efficient, scientific, *and* confidential.

He filed that possibility away for further consideration as talk turned to Nash's latest recruits, and they all headed for the treadmills.

∾

WITH THE NEXT curriculum committee's meeting just a week away, Delaney pulled up in front of Nash and Shelby's rambling farmhouse. Nash bought and fixed up the hundred-year-old farmhouse not long after he returned to Sterling to coach the football team, and Shelby moved in after Nash proposed.

Shelby sat in the porch swing, and waved at Delaney. "Come on up. I'm having a glass of lemonade. Want one?"

"Sounds good." Delaney climbed the steps, tote bag over her shoulder, as Shelby poured another glass.

"Nash is over in Decatur visiting his dad, so we have the afternoon to ourselves."

Nash's father, a former NFL quarterback, suffered from what they thought was chronic traumatic encephalopathy, or CTE, the result of years of quarterback sacks from defensive linemen the size of compact cars. Nash had moved him into a memory care facility last fall.

Delaney joined Shelby on the swing. "That's good. I need all the help I can get. With the exception of Dr. Burton, the committee members are a bunch of closed-minded old farts."

"We'll create a presentation that will knock their stodgy old socks off. First, let's talk about your approach, and then I can determine what data and graphs will wow the committee and make them wonder why they didn't just approve your major the first time around."

They talked things through while sipping refreshing lemonade then moved to Shelby's kitchen table. After another half hour of brainstorming, Shelby put the finishing touches on the colorful graphs, while Delaney watched in awe.

"You're a goddess. I don't know how you do that, but I'm thankful that you do."

Shelby clicked the mouse, moved some things around, changed the color scheme, then nodded. "Well, I don't know how people write romance novels, so we're even." Shelby turned the laptop screen so Delaney could see it better. "That should do it."

Studying the screen to make sure she understood the various graphs, she sighed, "If this doesn't convince even my worst critics, I don't know what will."

THE FIRST WEEK OF APRIL, Devon checked the time on his watch. He had just enough time to walk back to his office, pick up his notes, and head to the curriculum committee meeting where he would no doubt encounter the persistent Delaney Driscoll.

Picking up his French press coffee, he gathered his trash and walked over to the receptacle.

A bulletin board hung on the wall with flyers of all colors and sizes, advertising everything from the film department's Noir Night, to an upcoming production of Shakespeare on The Green, featuring *Twelfth Night*. The drama department's flyer hung at the top, and just below it, another flyer caught his eye.

ARE YOU OVER 18 AND SINGLE?
PARTICIPANTS WANTED FOR A STUDY.
COMPLETE A COMPATIBILITY QUESTIONNAIRE
AND A BLOOD DRAW.
FOR MORE INFORMATION

And it listed Dr. Samantha Love and her email address and phone number.

*Hmm.* He'd put the conversation about the study on the back burner, but it wouldn't hurt to sit down with her and ask a few questions. He glanced around to see if anyone was looking, then he tore off one of the tabs with her contact information, and stuck it in his pocket.

He surveyed the coffee shop once more, but no one seemed to notice him, so he headed for the door, an uncustomary spring in his step.

DELANEY TRIED to steady the pounding of her heart. She hadn't been this nervous since her dissertation defense, but after the March curriculum committee meeting, she knew she had an uphill battle with this group.

The committee had discussed five new courses, revisions to three programs, and one new major. They were getting crankier with each proposal. And hers was dead last on the agenda.

She looked at the clock on the wall above the committee chair's head. Time was running out. They'd given her ten minutes to present her information in support of her proposal, but if they didn't get to her soon, she wouldn't have time for even half of it.

Feeling eyes on her, she looked up and caught Devon's gaze. He nodded then returned his attention to Dr. Burton who was discussing the merits of the new engineering curriculum.

Five minutes left in the meeting. Biting her lip, she wondered if they would extend the time.

A vote was called on the engineering proposal, which passed the committee.

Dr. Gregors, the committee chair, finally addressed

Delaney. Thank goodness. "Dr. Driscoll, your proposal is next." He glanced up at the clock, a frown on his face.

"Dr. Gregors, if I may," Devon interjected. "Given the lack of time, I move that we table Dr. Driscoll's proposal until the next meeting."

Shelby stiffened and glared at Devon. What the–? *You've got to be kidding me!*

"I agree," Dr. Gregors said, then turned to Delaney. "I apologize. I had no idea the discussion of Dr. Bellinger's program revision would take so much time."

Delaney's heart sank. Another month before she could make her case.

And Devon had proposed it.

"I second the motion," Dr. Applebaum said.

"So moved."

*Dammit.* She glared at Devon, but he was making a note on the agenda.

*Great. Perfect.* She rose on shaky legs, biting back tears, not waiting for the vote. Silly. It wasn't as if she had a cure for cancer. It was just a romantic fiction degree. But it was her dream.

Suck it up, Driscoll. It could be worse. They could have voted against you once again.

DEVON STRODE out of the conference room, late for his next meeting when Delaney stepped in front of him, hands on her hips, eyes twin blue flames.

"You're such a jerk. Why did you do that?"

"Do what?" He didn't have time for this.

"Move to table my proposal?"

"Because we were out of time, and because some of us

have other meetings, like the one I'm currently late for." He gave her a look to say, *is that it?*

"Fine." She threw up her hands. "I'll just wait *another* month." She stomped off then spun back to face him. "This is so frustrating! I have all the information the committee asked for. I have data, and graphs, and–"

"And you deserve the time to present the full measure of your argument without being rushed."

She opened her mouth, closed it, then spoke. "Wait. What?"

His statement took the fire right out of her anger, and he struggled to keep the smirk off his face. "Delaney, don't you want adequate time to present all the work you put into your presentation?"

"Of course, but–"

"Then you should be happy I moved to table, rather than letting the committee push through their review your proposal, possibly denying it again."

"I–"

"Now, I really do have to get to this meeting." He brushed past her and could feel the confusion emanating from her.

Outside in the bright sunshine, he barked out a laugh. Score one for the jerk.

WHAT JUST HAPPENED?

Delaney stared after Devon's retreating back. Did he just do something *nice* for her? Again, just when she's written him off as the world's biggest jerk, he goes and does something considerate.

The door to the conference room opened and Dr.

Gregors came out, followed by a couple of the other committee members. "Oh, Delaney. Thank you for your patience. Devon suggested we put your proposal at the top of next month's agenda to ensure you have adequate time for your presentation. See you next month."

He fell in line with his colleagues as they walked toward the glass doors in Devon's wake.

Well, crap. He did it again.

Hard to hold a grudge against a guy who ruined it with his devious thoughtfulness.

**6**

———

Restless and out of sorts, Delaney paused the TV show she was currently binge-watching. An empty Ben & Jerry's container sat on the coffee table, along with a half-eaten bowl of popcorn.

Eight o'clock on a Friday night and here she was, sitting at home and feeling sorry for herself. Her usual emotional eating go-tos weren't quite upholding their end of the bargain. Lonely and bored—a lethal combination when it came to sensible eating.

Ethan and Sam were having dinner at his mother's, while Nash and Shelby had gone to visit his father in Decatur.

But even if her friends weren't otherwise occupied, she really needed to get a life. She couldn't be that friend who tagged along on date night and showed up at couples' dinners solo.

Throwing her head back against the couch cushions, she groaned.

"Enough."

Dying for some human contact besides the characters

from eighteenth-century Scotland, she cleaned up the detritus of her pity party and headed for her closet and something that would make her feel skinny. Fat chance—pun intended—especially after a pint of B&J's Chunky Monkey.

Sighing, she pulled on her black skinny jeans—they were somewhat slimming—and a red halter-top that made her girls look good. Some strappy stilettos boosted her self-confidence, along with her height.

A pat of blush, some mascara, and a swipe of red lip gloss, and she was out the door.

Shortly after, she entered McGinty's to find a good-sized crowd, but still a little early for the college students who didn't get their nights started until later. A couple vacated their seats at the bar, and Delaney snagged one of them, then caught the bartender's eye and ordered her favorite, a margarita.

Sipping from the salty rim, she turned to watch the couples dancing to a DJ's beats on the pub's stingy dance floor. She'd like to dance. If only someone would ask her. Scanning the room, she waved to a couple of professors from her college who were over by the dartboards.

Turning back to the bar with the intention of ordering some potato skins to soak up the tequila, she noticed someone slide onto the still-empty barstool next to her.

"Hi."

She glanced up in surprise to see a nice-looking guy, maybe in his mid-thirties, smiling at her. "Hi."

She didn't recognize him. Hair the color of a California surfer's fell over his forehead, giving him a boyish appearance. He had gray-blue eyes, a firm jaw with a subtle five o'clock shadow, and full lips meant for kissing, which she had no intention of doing. Checking out his left hand for signs of marriage, she smiled at the empty left ring finger. No telltale tan line either.

"This looks like a happening place," he said, his eyes scanning the pub before coming back to rest on her face.

"I gather you're not from here."

"No. Just visiting. I had an interview at the university, and may be moving here fulltime."

"Oh? What college?"

"Business."

Thinking of Devon and his perpetual frown, she lifted a brow. "Really? You don't strike me as the stuffed-shirt type."

He laughed. A nice, masculine chuckle. "I get that a lot. I'm Curtis, by the way, Curtis Michaels. Maybe you could show me around town."

"Well, Curtis, I'm Delaney," she responded as she held out her hand. She intentionally left off the last name. She was lonely, not stupid. "And maybe I could." They shook hands. It was nice. No zing, but it might be fun to hang out with him for the night, dance a little.

"Delaney, can I buy you a drink?"

"Sure." The evening was looking up. Maybe he'd even ask her to dance.

DEVON KNEW the moment Delaney entered the pub in those snug jeans that hugged her luscious curves. And that red top. Damn, she oozed sex! He choked for a second time in Delaney's presence, the scotch burning its way down his esophagus. Drinking and Delaney were a dangerous combination.

"You okay?"

Giving himself a mental head shake, he struggled to

return his attention to the conversation he was having with one of his department chairs.

"Yeah. Wrong pipe." They'd finished up a day of final interviews and negotiations with a candidate from Boston College and sought out McGinty's to both decompress and toast their success.

A few minutes later, the very same candidate joined Delaney at the bar. Devon sat up. A pick up? Or a pre-planned meeting?

"Why the frown?" Cal, his colleague asked.

"Was I frowning?" He glared into his highball glass, as disgust and anger bubbled to the surface.

"Still are," Cal said on a laugh then rose from the booth. "I'm calling it a night. Karen's making my favorite tonight— beef stroganoff. Thanks for the drink. I'll see you Monday."

Devon just nodded. Cal didn't notice their Golden Boy flirting with the sexiest woman in the pub.

The *married-with-two-kids* Golden Boy.

Devon drained his glass, intending to leave, until Golden Boy led Delaney out onto the dance floor. As he pulled her into him for a slow dance, a new emotion filled Devon. A heretofore unexperienced emotion.

Jealousy.

Completely irrational jealousy.

Grinding his teeth, he watched as Curtis' hands slowly inched down Delaney's back. When one hand touched her derrière, she reached back and returned it to a more respectable location then smiled and wagged her finger at him.

Curtis shrugged, a look of feigned chagrin on his face.

Devon would like to punch that fake chagrin right off his smug face.

Irrational jealousy aside, a philandering dirt bag did not

fit the culture he sought to create in his college. Talk about 'don't shit where you eat'! The guy thought he could have a fling with another university professor then move his wife and family here? The same family he'd waxed poetic about only three hours earlier?

*Oh, hell no.*

The official offer letter had not been presented because it required the provost's approval, but as far as Devon was concerned there would be no official offer.

Delaney laid a hand on Curtis' chest and Devon's stomach roiled. Then, with a flirtatious smile she headed toward the ladies' room.

Curtis licked his lips, his eyes on Delaney's ass, displayed to perfection in the snug denim, then he scanned the bar as if looking for witnesses. He'd made a mistake in thinking he had the all-clear when he followed Delaney to the back of the bar.

Should Devon follow? Or should he leave the matter be? No matter what he thought of Curtis' behavior, he and Delaney were adults.

But, did Delaney know he was married? He'd like to think she wouldn't intentionally pick up a married man in a bar. So, if she didn't know he was married, she'd be hurt that he'd led her on.

Mind made up, Devon strode through the crowded bar. Coming around the corner to the hallway leading to the bathrooms, he stopped short.

Curtis had Delaney pressed up against the wall, one leg thrust between hers, kissing her. The vision of Delaney in another man's arms hit him like a sucker punch to the stomach. Through a red haze of anger and jealousy, Devon took out his cellphone and snapped a picture. Exhibit A in his decision not to hire Curtis.

Just as he'd decided to walk away, Delaney's hands shoved against Curtis' shoulders. "No! Stop it!" She wasn't trying to pull him closer, she was trying to get away.

"Come on, baby," Curtis said on a laugh. "You don't have to play hard to get with me. I know you want it." His hand slid up, groping her breast.

And Devon snapped. "Back off, asshole!"

CURTIS BACKED AWAY, a smug expression on his face, his hands up in surrender, until he saw the source of the command. The jerk went from smug to horrified in a millisecond.

Delaney was just as shocked as Curtis to see Devon standing there, his jaw set, his eyes stony, but why Curtis' reaction?

Devon stepped in front of Delaney, putting himself between her and Curtis. "'No' means 'no.' And in this case, 'no' also means 'no job offer.'"

*Job offer?* Of course, she thought, the College of Business.

"You can't do that." Curtis stepped into Devon. "You've already made the offer."

Devon held up his phone. "I think your wife and family will have something to say in the matter."

Stunned, and a little sick, Delaney cried, "You're *married*?"

Curtis went white. "You wouldn't."

"Try me." Devon ground out.

"Bitch asked for it," he muttered.

Delaney gasped and staggered back. She'd done no such thing. She'd only wanted a dance and some conversation with a smart, nice-looking guy.

When she saw him standing in the hallway, she'd thought he'd come out of the men's room, but when he pushed her into the wall, she realized he'd been waiting for her.

"Get out, before I have Hugh toss your sorry ass out."

"I wouldn't want to live in this uptight town anyway." As Delaney watched Curtis stomp off, her knees suddenly went weak.

Devon glared after Curtis then turned to Delaney. "Are you all right?"

She nodded.

"No, you're not. You're trembling." He removed his suit jacket and draped it over her shoulders. Only Devon Mayfield would be at a pub on a Friday night wearing a suit and tie. The warmth of his jacket enveloped her, making her shiver in response. Then his sexy, spicy scent invaded her senses, and she drew in a deep, calming breath.

He rubbed her arms, warming her. "Come on. Let me see you home."

"I'm fine."

"Says every woman who's really not."

She took a step back, and her knee buckled. *Okay, so maybe not fine.*

Devon wrapped her hand into the crook of his arm and escorted her through the crowded bar as if escorting her to a ball. She ignored the *zing* his touch elicited.

Once outside, she took another deep, calming breath. *What a night.* She would have been better off staying home and polishing off another pint of ice cream.

"Where's your car?"

"I walked."

"You *what*?" he growled, as he turned to face her.

"It's safe."

"You mean like McGinty's is safe?"

She huffed out an exasperated sigh. "Fine."

"Come with me." He wrapped an arm around her waist.

"Where are we going?"

"I'm driving you home."

"But I only live five blocks from here." She pointed in the direction of her apartment. "We can walk."

"We'll apologize to the environment later," he muttered as he led her to a metallic silver car–

"A Tesla? Guess you don't need to apologize to the environment after all," she muttered.

He held open the car door for her, and she slid into the butter-soft leather seat. Classy, just like Devon. And environmentally friendly. Who knew?

*How much did a college dean make anyway?*

When they were both sealed inside the noise-cancelling passenger compartment, her pulse kicked up a notch. And not with fear. The quiet intimacy, the warmth of his jacket, and the scent of him formed a deadly mix, making her hyperaware of the man next to her.

No. Not fear. He might be a first-class jerk when it came to her curriculum proposal, but she knew in her bones he wouldn't turn into an octopus-with-a-dick like Curtis.

She felt his eyes on her. "What?"

"Your address?"

Licking her dry lips, she replied. "Oh. Right." She rattled off the address, and he backed out of the parking space.

It took all of about two minutes to reach her apartment. When he pulled up out front, she turned to him. "I was about to knee him in the family jewels when you showed up." She continued, "But thank you for stepping in."

She didn't know why she felt the need to explain herself to Devon, but she did. "I only wanted to dance. Not to . . ."

"Of course." He stared out the windshield, saying nothing more. The night's scene played on a loop in his head—Delaney in the arms of another man; Delaney unsuccessfully trying to shove the man off her. And every time the loop played, two emotions warred inside him: jealousy and anger.

Jealousy was a strange, new emotion for him. And he didn't care for it. As for the anger, any man worth his gentleman card would have been pissed to see an unwilling woman struggling against an unwanted embrace.

"He's joining the faculty at Sterling?"

Her question drew him back to the present. "Not anymore."

"Because of me?" her voice sounded small in the quiet car.

"No. Because of no one but himself."

"I didn't know he was married," she added.

"I gathered."

"And he has children?"

"Two. A three-year-old daughter and an eight-month-old son."

She pressed a hand to her stomach.

He finally allowed himself to look at her. "Are you sure you're okay?"

"Why wouldn't I be?"

"You were just . . . assaulted–"

She waved her hand, brushing off the seriousness of the night's episode. "It wasn't the first time something like that has happened, and I'm sure it won't be the last. Men see my body and think I'm all about sex. And that I'm more than willing to give that sex away. I'm used to it," she finished, with a resigned sigh.

He shifted in his seat to face her. "There's no excuse for that kind of behavior," he said. That Delaney believed that the Neanderthal behavior she apparently experienced on a regular basis was something to be shrugged off sickened him. She deserved so much more respect than that.

Not that Delaney was in any way . . . special to him. Of course, he would feel the same about any woman.

At least, that's what he told himself.

"You're right. But there will always be jerks out there just the same." Opening the door, she climbed out. "Well, thank you again."

"Delaney?"

She ducked her head inside the car. "Yes?"

"My jacket."

"Oh. Right. Thanks for that too."

He watched as she walked up to her door then turned to wave, signaling that he could go.

She closed the car door behind her, leaving the scent of her perfume behind.

Devon leaned his forehead against the steering wheel. Being in close contact with Delaney Driscoll was dangerous for his peace of mind.

**7**

───────

As Sam laid out the items for his blood test, Devon read over the consent form.

It stated that participants would be notified if there was a match with someone in the database, provided the match had also agreed to be contacted. Good. He could get the results, and not have to go through the undignified process of an online dating site. He did have one very important question though.

"Are the individuals in your database only local?" So far he hadn't met anyone in Sterling who would meet his, er, professional needs. Delaney came to mind, but the needs she would meet were far from professional.

"No. I have participants from all over the country."

Convinced, he picked up the pen and scrawled his name across the bottom of the document.

"Ready?" she asked.

"Yes," he replied. She swabbed his finger with alcohol. "Ethan said the two of you were a match."

A shy smile lit her face and she blushed. Yet, she didn't strike him as the blushing type. "We were."

That was encouraging. Anyone could see they were the perfect partnership. Smart, successful, supportive. If he could find such a match, he could put the next step of his plan into action.

"How are you settling into your new position at the college?" Sam asked, as she wrapped a Band-Aid around his index finger.

"I'm still learning who hates who."

She laughed. "That's always a good first step in a new job, especially when that job involves managing people." She glanced up at him again, as if she had something else to say, then hesitated.

"What?"

She shook her head.

"Just say it."

"It's not really my place."

"But?"

"But. Delaney's proposal." She gathered up the trash. "She may not be scientific or data-driven like we are, but Delaney's smart. Her students adore her. And she's worked hard creating the major. She's done her research, not only on the best courses but on the romantic fiction market too."

Unsure what to say, he didn't respond. He'd tried, albeit unsuccessfully, to get Delaney off his mind all weekend, and here, Sam brings her up in conversation.

"Well, as I said, it's not my place. You need to log on to this website and take the compatibility questionnaire." She handed him a card. "This card has your unique code and password. Once you've completed the questionnaire, hit 'submit.' Your responses upload to my database with your unique code so I can match it to your blood test results."

Devon took the card from her and stuck it in his pocket. "I'll do it tonight."

"There's no rush. It will likely take me a year to complete enrollment on my study."

While she was in no hurry, Devon was. The sooner he found his mate, the sooner he could pursue his goals. And the sooner he could get Delaney off his mind.

THE FOLLOWING THURSDAY, Devon rubbed his eyes then gazed out the window to the Campus Quad three stories below. He'd spent the last several hours shuffling papers and responding to emails. His eyes deserved a break.

His butt likely deserved one too. A walk to Uncommon Grounds would fit the bill.

Just as he rose from his seat, an email popped up on his computer screen. He groaned and sat back down. Then his stomach did a backflip when he read the subject line: MATCH FOUND.

His hand hovered over the mouse. This could be it. But what if she lived in Oregon, or California, and had no desire to move to a small university town in Northeast Georgia? Or, what if she'd already found someone? Someone who wasn't her histocompatible mate because she'd given up? Sam warned that this could happen. That there were no guaranties.

He rose from his chair again and rounded his desk. It was lunchtime, and Rachel was probably out of the office, but he closed his door anyway. Returning to his chair, he pulled it up to the keyboard, took a deep breath, and opened the email.

DEAR DR. MAYFIELD,

We are pleased to inform you that your blood test results matched to an individual in our database. This individual agreed to the release of her name in the event of any histocompatible matches. You will find the information on this individual in the attached document, including her name, age, and contact information. If you desire to contact this person, or if this person chooses to contact you, this is not handled by the research team.

As always, if you have any questions, please feel free to contact the study investigator, Dr. Samantha Love.

The Study Team

He clicked on the attachment and quickly scanned it, sitting back in stunned silence. The name of his histocompatible mate: Delaney Driscoll.

"This can't be right. Can it? Tell me it's not right." Delaney held up a copy of the email she'd printed just this morning.

Sam smiled. Well, smirked really. "It's right. You and Devon Mayfield are a match."

"That's not what you were supposed to say." Delaney sank into the guest chair in Sam's office. "But. No." She shook her head. "It can't be."

Even as she said it, she couldn't deny the intensity of the chemistry between them. Even when he pissed her off, she wondered what it would be like to kiss him.

Nevertheless–

Sam stood and walked around her desk, perching on the

front edge. "I don't have to remind you I thought the same thing about Ethan—and it was *my* research."

Delaney stared up at Sam, still a little dumbfounded, but remembered Sam's reaction when she learned that, according to her love test, she and her now-fiancé were a match. She chose at first not to believe her own science, leading to an existential crisis of sorts.

Because if Sam believed in her science, it should follow that she would believe Ethan was her perfect histocompatible mate. And that, according to her research, histocompatible mates make the happiest relationships.

If she didn't believe Ethan was her perfect mate, it would bring into question her research. Her compatibility assay. Her reputation. Not to mention her very career.

Delaney really wanted to be supportive of her friend by supporting her science, but believing that the broody, Darcy-like Devon Mayfield was her perfect match was a bridge too far. Even if Mr. Darcy was her favorite literary character.

And even if, like Mr. Darcy, he did surprisingly nice things sometimes.

She glanced up at Sam who was patiently waiting for her to accept the results and move on.

But–

"You know I love you and respect your work, but this," she lifted the now-crumpled email, "I just can't go there." Even if he is the hottest thing she'd seen in a very long time.

Sam shrugged and rose to walk back around her desk. "Suit yourself."

"Does he know?"

"If not yet, he will soon. His email went out the same time yours did."

Delaney closed her eyes and groaned. "He'll think this is

some kind of set-up. Maybe a way to get back at him for his opposition to my proposal."

"Yeah, because finding his perfect mate is the ideal revenge," Sam replied, her voice laced with sarcasm.

"No offense, but this is preposterous." Devon pointed to the email he'd summarily laid on Sam's desk.

"Déjà vu," Sam muttered to herself.

"What?"

"Nothing." Sam shook her head. "And none taken. Been there," she said with a grin. "No one else knows but you and me. And Delaney, of course. What the two of you decide to do with the information is up to you, but you'll see it's right in the end."

"A foregone conclusion then?" He eyed her. "She's your friend. Correction, she's your *single* friend. Who's to say you two didn't cook this scheme up?"

She glared at him. "Okay, now I'm offended."

He rubbed his brow. "You're right, that was insulting. I apologize."

"And for what possible purpose would we cook up such a scheme?" Sam continued.

"To get her married off, of course." He threw up his hand as if to say, 'Isn't it obvious?'

"Devon, this isn't Regency England. People marry whomever they choose to. Even my test results can't *make* you marry someone you don't believe is a match for you."

"Believe?"

"Yes. If you don't believe the results, there is nothing I, or Delaney for that matter, can do."

"You're talking as if I should believe in the results like

children believe in Santa Claus, the Tooth Fairy, or the Easter Bunny. Is this science, or is this make-believe?"

"Oh, it's science. But not everyone believes in science. Even when the evidence is irrefutable."

*Irrefutable?*

He'd been restless and out of sorts since that first day Delaney introduced herself in McGinty's, unable to focus on his plan both for the college and for his life, but especially his love life. He snorted. *Love life?* Where had that come from?

Devon Mayfield didn't do love. Or, if he was brutally honest with himself, love didn't do him.

"If it makes you feel any better, she's not thrilled either."

His head snapped up. "What?"

"She's in the same boat as you—floating down Denial River."

He snorted. "Denial?"

"Yes. She doesn't want to believe you're her match, either."

*Delaney* didn't want *him*? Good. Fine. It was for the best.

Rejection wasn't a new emotion for him. He'd already experienced it from the one person in the world who should love and accept him without reservation.

Then why did learning about Delaney's rejection make his chest tighten?

THE FOLLOWING MORNING, after a night spent tossing and turning, Devon slipped into Delaney's classroom planning to confront her afterward with the test results. Nip this thing in the bud.

While Sam said Delaney wasn't happy about the results

either, he wanted to see for himself and clear up any potential for confusion on her part. They were not a perfect match, science be damned.

He closed the door at the back of the classroom with a soft click and slid into an empty seat in the last row.

Delaney stood at the front of the compact theater-style classroom, an open book in one hand as she paced. With her blond hair pulled back into a high ponytail and her pin-up girl body displayed to perfection in a colorful dress that wrapped around her curves and tied at the waist, she made it difficult for him to remember his mission this morning.

The guys whose faces he could see stared at her, lust written all over their faces. And he had an irrational desire to blindfold them all.

But he also noticed that every female student was engaged in the discussion. Not a single laptop screen displayed solitaire, Instagram, or Twitter. They were opened to word-processing programs filled with notes.

Delaney caught sight of him and frowned before continuing her lecture. "When Othello enters the bedchamber, he doesn't know whether to kill Desdemona or go all *Fifty Shades* on her."

The class laughed, and a student raised her hand. "Why doesn't he just wait to see if Desdemona cheated on him?"

"What would be the fun in that? Then there would be no tragedy, and I wouldn't be torturing you with a play Shakespeare wrote over four hundred years ago."

The class laughed again.

"All right, time's up. Don't forget, your papers are due next Monday."

A collective groan spread through the thirty-some-odd students as they packed up their laptops and books. A few walked down the steps to talk with Delaney. She smiled, her blue eyes alight with pleasure. Nodding, she listened intently to what a petite brunette was saying, then Delaney giggled and pulled her in for a hug. Clearly her students admired and respected her, and the feeling was mutual. Delaney stepped back then lifted her closed hand for a fist bump.

Before everyone exited, Delaney called for their attention.

"Congratulate Bethany here. She just received a small private grant to attend Oxford University this summer for a special program on Jane Austen."

Bethany's fellow classmates clapped and cheered, as she waved them off, blushing.

Devon waited for the last of the students to exit then made his way down the steps to the lectern.

Closing her laptop, Delaney tucked it into a tote bag that read: THE PAST, THE PRESENT, AND THE FUTURE WALKED INTO A BAR. IT WAS TENSE.

"Slumming, Dr. Mayfield?"

"What?"

"I never thought you would deign to enter the world of literature."

He snorted. Guess he deserved that. "I like Shakespeare. Even if I don't always understand it."

"Was that a self-deprecating remark?"

He shoved his hands in his pockets and shrugged.

"Well, what can I do for you?"

Now that she stood in front of him, he hesitated to broach the subject. "I don't suppose you received an email yesterday?"

Delaney shouldered the tote bag and turned to him. "And what email would that be?"

Devon sighed. So this was how she was going to play it.

"The email from Sam that said," he pulled a hand out of his pocket and waved the piece of paper between them, "we're a match."

"Oh, *that* email." She put a finger to her chin in feigned thought. "Come to think of it, I think I saw something like that in my junk mail."

*Junk mail?* "So, you don't–"

"Believe it? No."

He nodded. "Good."

Her head snapped up as she narrowed her eyes at him. "Good?"

"Yes. I mean, Sam is your friend, so I'm sure you have a great deal of confidence in her science, but I wouldn't want you to get the impression that we were headed for the altar or anything."

"The altar?" She gave a rueful laugh. "Don't flatter yourself, Dr. Mayfield. You're not my type."

"And what type is that?" he asked, unable to keep the defensive tone out of his voice.

She tilted her head as if considering him as a potential mate. His back itched between his shoulder blades as he got the distinct impression that she found him lacking. An all-too-familiar feeling.

"Men with a heart." She breezed past him, her perfume enveloping him in a cloud of sweet seduction.

"That went well," he muttered as he watched her climb the steps. "So glad we understand one another."

Even so, his heart felt like lead in his chest.

**8**

───────

The following Friday evening, Delaney stretched out on a blanket, legs crossed at the ankles, hands behind her back propping herself up. Next to her, the lovebirds held hands or cuddled on their own blankets. She'd hear the occasional smooch, further deepening her morose thoughts.

Good thing tonight's Shakespeare on the Green was *Twelfth Night* and not *Hamlet*. Otherwise, the tragedy might tempt her to follow Ophelia's lead and drown herself in the nearest brook.

If she had to match with someone in Sam's database, why'd it have to be Devon Mayfield?

She could admit a touch of split personality disorder when it came to Devon Mayfield. He tried her patience, challenged her views, kept her constantly off-balance with his Dr. Jekyll/Mr. Hyde act all rolled into one sexy package. And wasn't that just the problem?

Too damn sexy for his own good. Or hers, for that matter.

Popping a grape into her mouth, she grimaced at the

sour taste. *Perfect.* Even the grapes were souring from her mood. Well, she thought, as she lifted her cup of wine, if the grapes didn't make her feel better, maybe their fermented juice would.

The Green, the former site of the Sterling estate's tennis courts and croquet green, sat on the southwest corner of campus enclosed by a wall of six-foot Burford holly hedges. Several years ago, when a wealthy donor gave the university a generous gift to build a small amphitheater that could be used for performances by the school's drama, music, and dance departments, they'd torn up the tennis courts, graded the land, and built the amphitheater.

The university also rented out the venue for concerts and other theatrical productions, creating a funding source to support the College of Arts and Sciences' programs. The venue had become a popular spot for entertainment all through the spring, summer, and fall months.

"There he is," Ethan said, drawing Delaney's attention. *There who is?*

She got her answer when she looked up to see the source of her aggravation standing behind them, a bottle of wine in one hand, his other in the pocket of his khaki pants and a frown gracing his face. Nothing new there.

And didn't the man own a pair of jeans?

"Join us," Ethan said, indicating Delaney's blanket. *What the–?*

Ethan had invited Devon to the play then expected Delaney to share her blanket with him?

She caught Sam's eye, but she shrugged at Delaney's incredulous expression.

"Thanks, I'll just sit over here." He nodded to a spot a few paces to Delaney's left, where he'd have to sit on the grass.

Sighing, she moved over, giving him room between her and the lovebirds. "Come on, there's plenty of room." She patted the blanket.

"You sure?"

"Yes. You can't sit on the grass. You'll get your pants dirty." She released a sigh that said, *Silly man, don't you know grass stains are a bitch to get out?*

"Thanks." He stretched out next to her, careful to hug the edge of the blanket.

Rolling her eyes, she said, "I won't bite, you know."

"No, I don't know."

She snorted. "I never thought you'd come to a Shakespeare play," Delaney prodded. "You know, with your hatred of literature and everything." She gave him a broad smile.

"I never said I hated literature. I told you, I like literature and Shakespeare as much as the next person."

"So you say. You just don't like romance."

"I never said that either." He sounded exasperated. "I just don't think there is any value in a major for romance writers."

"Tell that to the more than nine thousand members of Romance Writers of America. Did you know that romance novels share more than thirty-four percent of the U.S. fiction market? That–"

"Wine?" Ethan held out a cup of the merlot they'd been drinking, interrupting Delaney's tirade. She cut a glance his way, and he gave a subtle head shake. She huffed. *Fine.* So now wasn't the time.

Devon took the cup and nodded his thanks.

"There's crackers, cheese, and fruit too." Sam supplied, also giving Delaney a look that said, *Don't swat at the hornet's nest.* "We'll set out dinner during intermission."

"Sounds good." He rose to his knees and reached for a small plate, loading it with appetizers.

Eyeing his plate, Delaney asked after he'd stretched out again, "Hungry?"

He glanced up at her, the corner of his mouth curving, flashing a tiny dimple in his cheek, then he set the plate between them. "I thought you might like something as well."

"Oh. Thanks." Well, that was . . . thoughtful. Dammit.

Musicians dressed in sixteenth-century garb entered the stage playing flutes, and a hush fell over the audience.

"It's starting," Delaney whispered.

The Duke Orsino entered, attended by his lords, and recited the famous opening line: "If music be the food of love, play on."

Delaney closed her eyes and let the words wash over her. One of her favorite Shakespeare plays, *Twelfth Night* tells the story of Viola, who is in love with Orsino, who is in love with Olivia, who is in love with Viola's male disguise, Cesario. This love triangle is complicated by the fact that neither Orsino nor Olivia knows that Viola is, in fact, a woman pretending to be Cesario.

It's the stuff of a perfect romantic comedy.

But, as the play progressed, Delaney found herself distracted by the man lying on the blanket next to her. Even with hundreds of other people around her, the arrangement felt intimate, especially since night had fallen.

His cologne, the now-familiar warm, spicy scent, drifted her way on the breeze. They both reached for something on the plate at the same time, and their hands touched, sending a jolt up her arm. He must have felt it too because he jerked his hand back. "You first," he whispered, his voice holding a rusty quality to it.

"No. I'm good." She directed her attention back to the stage.

Later, she adjusted her position, and her hand landed directly on top of Devon's. Another now-familiar jolt ran up her arm, and she sat up, resisting the urge to shake her hand as if shocked. "Sorry."

As Sir Andrew, Sir Toby, and Maria headed off to watch Malvolio make a buffoon of himself, a court jester stepped forward to announce a fifteen-minute intermission, and Delaney breathed a sigh of relief. She needed to distance herself from the infuriating, superior, and—*dammit*—appealing Devon Mayfield. ASAP.

"Bathroom," she muttered, as she headed off in that direction. Any port in a storm, even if that port was a Porta-Potty.

DEVON WATCHED Delaney pick her way around lawn chairs and blankets, picnic baskets and coolers, until the darkness swallowed her up.

What had he been thinking? He should have turned down Ethan's invitation to join them. Naturally, Delaney would be with them.

Hyperaware of the woman next to him, he couldn't concentrate on the play. Shakespeare was difficult enough to follow when given his undivided attention, but with Delaney's scent and warmth, not to mention her sultry giggles when a comedic line was recited, he'd become completely lost.

He might as well have been watching a play performed in Polish.

Then there were Delaney's silky legs, displayed to

perfection in the deep pink dress she wore, and her dainty feet with their bright purple toenail polish.

As the audience prepared to dine on cold fried chicken, sandwiches, or salads, lights flickered on across The Green. Camp lanterns, battery-operated candles, flashlights, and cell phones provided light.

"Devon, what would you like?" Sam interrupted his thoughts. "We have a cold salmon-and-cucumber salad, Shelby's homemade potato salad, Ruby's cold fried chicken, a green salad, and for dessert, Delaney's chocolate pie."

He should have guessed a dessert as sinful as chocolate pie would come from Delaney. Sin on a plate, just like her. "I'll take a little of everything, thanks."

Delaney breezed past him, her orange-blossom scent driving him nuts. When she sat back down on the blanket, her skirt floated up, giving him a flash of smooth thigh and bright pink panties, and he nearly groaned out loud.

She crossed her legs yoga-style, draped her dress over her lap, and reached for a plate, before kneeling and helping herself to the green and salmon salads. He almost swallowed his tongue when her delicious ass hovered near his face.

If this damnable play didn't end soon, he'd have to make an early exit in order to avoid embarrassing himself with his physical reaction.

THE ACTORS CAME out for their curtain calls as the audience stood and applauded, a few 'bravos' coming from the crowd. *Thank God.* Not that the performance had been bad—it had been quite good. That is, when he could actually concentrate on it.

But sitting in close proximity to Delaney for over two and a half hours was akin to dangling a carrot in front of a starving rabbit, but not letting the creature have it.

The empty wine bottles, leftovers, dirty dishes, blankets, and lawn chairs had been packed away, and the patrons began making their way to their cars or bicycles.

"Not too bad for small-town living, right, Devon?" Ethan asked.

"I had a good time. Thanks for the invitation."

"Any time. Delaney, can we walk you to your car?"

"Oh, I walked. Thanks, though."

*Walked?* Again?

"We'll give you a lift then," Ethan continued.

"I'm fine. Really."

"Del, I don't think so," Sam shook her head.

"I'll see that she gets home," Devon interjected. Why, he didn't know. Except he couldn't allow a woman to walk home alone at night, even if the town seemed safe. At Delaney's frown, he continued, "I insist."

"Thank you, Devon," Sam said. "I feel better."

He nodded and cut a glance at Delaney. If looks could kill . . . Maybe he should be concerned for his own safety instead.

Indicating that he would follow her lead, he waited for her to say her goodnights and then fell into step beside her. The temperature had dropped, and clouds scudded across the dark sky. Delaney shrugged into a sweater and pulled it tight, crossing her arms over her body.

They walked in an uncomfortable silence across The Green toward downtown Sterling.

Clearing his throat, he broke the silence. "What's with you and walking?"

"It's good for the environment, and it's healthy. But don't

worry, it's just a few blocks. You won't be stuck escorting me for too long."

Heaving an exasperated sigh, he said, "It's no hardship."

Her head snapped in his direction, a look of surprise on her face.

"Despite what you may think of me, Delaney, I have no ill feelings toward you."

"As long as I'm not trying to drag you to the altar or implement a major in romantic fiction." She shook her head.

They walked in silence for a time. A light rain began to fall.

"Perfect," Delaney muttered.

"You cold?" Devon asked, cutting a glance her way.

"I'm fine."

He rolled his eyes. "Come here." He put an arm around her shoulder and tucked her up against him. She stiffened then snuggled closer into his warmth wrapping an arm around his waist, and his brain momentarily short-circuited at the contact.

A few tense minutes later, she stopped in front of her apartment complex, and stepped away from him. "This is me."

He hadn't paid much attention when he'd previously dropped her off—he'd still been seeing red over Curtis' animalistic behavior. The apartments were attractive, with red-brick façades, black shutters, and red doors giving them a Georgian aesthetic, not uncommon in the Deep South.

"You're dismissed, Dr. Mayfield." She smirked. "You have fulfilled your obligation to see me home."

"My obligation isn't over until I see you to your door."

She tilted her head, her hair damp from the rain. "This isn't the inner city, Devon."

"Even so." He held out his hand for her to precede of him.

They arrived at her doorstep. "Mission accomplished," she said, with a sharp heel-click and a salute.

She'd accented her front door with clay pots filled with a riot of colorful flowers. A doormat with a yellow-brick-road graphic read: YOU'RE NOT IN KANSAS ANYMORE. Remembering her bio on the university's website, he couldn't help but smile at that.

When he looked up, her eyes held his, and the air between them crackled. He had the inexplicable urge to kiss her. Absurd. This hadn't been a date. And she'd made it clear that the sooner they parted, the better.

"Goodnight, Delaney."

Delaney inserted her key in the lock. "Goodnight, Devon."

He hiked back through the rain, the memory of Delaney's curves keeping him warm all the way back to his car.

9

_____

The quaint downtown area streets were closed to vehicular traffic, and tents lined both sides, artists displaying everything from paintings to jewelry and pottery to quilts. They'd gotten a lucky break with the weather, after a week of cold, drizzly rain.

But with the passing of the rain, spring had sprung in all its glory. The trees lining Main Street sported bright green leaves, tulips and hyacinths vied for space in the planters along the sidewalks, and the air was warm and fragrant.

Devon didn't generally have an interest in art festivals, but with weather too inviting to stay indoors, it was as good an excuse as any to enjoy the fresh air and bright sunshine.

The scent of funnel cakes, mixed with grilling meats, kettle corn, and roasted nuts, created an appetizing cornucopia of smells.

He nodded to an acquaintance from the university, sidestepped two dogs who greeted one another like long-lost friends, and then caught a glimpse of a curvy blonde in a spring-green dress up ahead. He'd recognize that body anywhere. The feel of it pressed against his side last Friday night was indelibly imprinted on his memory.

She meandered along, stopping at tents, talking with the artists, her smile so bright, she competed with the sun. In one hand she held a bag, and in the other an ice cream cone, her purse over her shoulder. In that moment, she looked young and innocent. But as the breeze flirted with her skirt, the image the glimpse of bare leg conjured was far from innocent.

He finally caught up to her and couldn't decide whether to leave her be or acknowledge her.

When she turned and spotted him, she made the decision for him.

"Delaney."

"Devon." She nodded then took another lick of her melting ice cream cone, and dear God, he felt it like a hot dart to the groin.

He hadn't spotted her friends. "Are you here alone?"

"Yes. You?"

"Yes."

Awkward pause. He cleared his throat. "You, uh, mind if I join you?"

She shrugged. "Sure."

He fell in beside her, interested in what artists drew her attention. "Where are your sidekicks?"

She grinned at the moniker. "Shelby and Nash are visiting Shelby's mother in Miami, and Sam and Ethan left for a conference in San Francisco where Sam is speaking."

She stopped in front of a tent displaying delicately wrought jewelry pieces, some with tiny gemstones, others with pearls. He could see her wearing many of the items on display. They suited her blatant femininity. After a few minutes of browsing, she complimented the artist and they moved on. She'd polished off the ice cream cone and paused to toss the napkins in the trash.

Next stop—a tent displaying breathtaking photos of far-away places he hoped to someday visit. The next—a tent with enormous colorful canvases painted with broad, confident strokes.

"Which do you prefer, photographs or paintings?" he asked, as they stood in front of a red, orange, pink, and yellow abstract piece that reminded him of a sunset.

She considered the question a moment before responding. "While I appreciate the skill and talent of a painting, I prefer photographs. They capture the beauty in the world for that one moment in time. Nature photographers, especially, don't get to pick their compositions. They see it in the blink of an eye and have to capture it before it's gone." She'd responded to his question without looking at him, staring at the sunset painting.

Very astute. "I agree. I have some walls in my new home in need of some art. Perhaps I'll purchase something here today."

"You should. Support the arts and the artists who create them."

He pointed to her bag. "Is that what you're doing?"

"Yes. And because I like what I see." She exited the tent, and he followed.

She stopped in front of a portraitist, the subject of his drawing a little girl squirming in a chair a few feet away. "Mom, can I see it yet?"

"Not yet. Sit still. The sooner you sit still, the sooner he can finish, and the sooner you can see it."

The artist showed skill. He'd managed to capture the precocious little elf in just a few strokes of charcoal.

The mom paid, handed her little girl the drawing, and thanked the artist.

"How about you, ma'am? Would you like a portrait?" he asked Delaney, an expectant look on his bearded face.

"Sure," she said with a shrug. "Why not." Sitting in the chair, she flipped her hair back and cast a flirtatious grin over her shoulder, looking both sultry and innocent at the same time.

The artist made quick work of the drawing, capturing the alluring dimple in her right cheek, the curve of her upper lip, the arch of her eyebrows. But more than that, he captured her sunshine.

When the artist revealed the final drawing to her, she clapped her hands and laughed. "I love it. Thank you."

She dug in her purse and handed him the fee plus a large tip.

"Thank you, ma'am. Much appreciated."

Delaney gave Devon a shoulder nudge. "Your turn."

"What?" Devon glanced up from the drawing, startled. "No."

"Oh, come on." She indicated the chair. "Support the arts and the artists who create them," she said with a smirk.

"Fine." Sighing heavily, Devon sank to the hard metal folding chair, feeling incredibly self-conscious as the artist worked to render his likeness in charcoal, Delaney standing over the artist's shoulder with a sly smile on her face.

A few short, uncomfortable minutes later, the artist handed him the drawing.

Devon stared at the portrait of himself. *Hmm.* Did he really look like that?

"Wow! He captured you perfectly. All broody and grumpy." Delaney gave him another shoulder nudge.

"I'm not broody. I don't brood."

"The gentleman doth protest too much, methinks," she admonished with a wink.

He examined the picture with a critical eye. *Huh.* Maybe she was right.

Devon handed money to the artist.

*A fifty! Holy cow.* Delaney's mouth dropped open, and the artist's eyes nearly bugged out of his head. "Thank you, sir."

Devon nodded then rolled up his drawing, binding it with a rubber band from the grateful artist.

As they walked away, she leaned in and whispered, "You do realize you just gave the man a fifty, right?"

"Of course."

*Well then.* Big spender.

Dressed in navy slacks and a white button-down, Devon was his usual buttoned-up self.

"Can I ask you a question?"

He tensed next to her. "Yes. I think."

"Don't you own a pair of jeans?" She thought she caught a glimmer of a smile, but she must have been mistaken.

"I'm sure there's a pair somewhere in my closet. Why?"

"You should wear them sometime. You always look so . . . unapproachable."

His steps faltered, and his eyebrows shot up, but that was the extent of his reaction.

She paused in front of a tent displaying what appeared to be hand-drawn book covers of literary classics like *Jane Eyre, Anna Karenina, A Christmas Carol, Huckleberry Finn,* and, her favorite, *Pride and Prejudice.* So unique.

"These are beautiful." She reverently touched a framed

print. Most appeared to be of the original first edition covers. The artist had clearly done his or her homework. They'd look wonderful in her office.

Peering at the price tag, disappointment sank in. Pricey. Not that she could blame the artist. The work was detailed, and no doubt time-consuming. Even so. While she could appreciate the time, energy, and skill that went into the drawings, she couldn't afford even one of them.

"See something you like?"

Delaney turned and gazed into the smiling eyes of a woman in bohemian dress with long flowing gray hair.

"Everything?" Delaney laughed. "Are these yours?"

"Yes."

"You do exquisite work."

"Thank you."

"You enjoy the classics?"

"Yes. And I enjoy researching the first-edition covers and bringing them back to life." She handed a brochure to Delaney and Devon.

"Well, you've done an amazing job. I wish I could afford one for my office."

The artist smiled. "I understand."

Delaney felt Devon's presence and glanced over her shoulder. He wore a frown as he studied the brochure. Probably bored stiff.

"Maybe another time," Delaney said as she exited the tent, Devon right behind her.

"It's early, but I skipped lunch. How about some dinner?" He stopped in front of a kettle corn vendor, and the scent made her stomach growl.

"Dr. Mayfield, are you asking me to dinner?"

"Yes. But it's not a date."

She laughed. "Heaven forbid."

He smiled. Or at least she thought it was a smile. A slight lift of the right corner of his mouth. Or maybe it was a twitch. Probably a twitch.

"To what do I owe this honor?" Delaney prodded.

"No honor. Just an olive branch."

"Oh? What for?"

"I think we got off on the wrong foot."

"You mean first by you voting against my proposal, and second by insulting me with your insinuation that I'm a gold digger? Does this mean you've changed your mind about my curriculum proposal?"

"Not unless you change it for me. But that doesn't mean we can't be friends."

"Oh." A strange man Devon Mayfield was. "Sure." She shrugged. They'd spent this much time together without killing each other. Maybe they could get through dinner.

Devon held open the door of Ruby's, indicating she should precede him.

"You said 'friends.' But friends support one another. Stick up for one another. Don't vote against their friends' hopes and dreams."

Ruby's was doing a brisk business with patrons from the art show. The lunch counter resembled something out of the 1950s. Red vinyl stools, Formica countertop, stainless-steel trim. An old jukebox stood in the corner, playing Frankie Valle. The booth, with its red vinyl upholstery beckoned for the cast of *Happy Days*.

As they waited for the besieged staff to help them, Devon continued, "Hopes and dreams? Delaney, think about this logically. The curriculum committee can't just approve a new degree because it's someone's hope or dream."

Delaney rolled her eyes. "That's not what I'm saying."

"There's not enough data to support approving the degree program."

Mandy, one of the servers, looked harried as she carried a tray weighed down with food across the black-and-white-checkered linoleum floor. The tantalizing aroma of Ruby's meatloaf reached Delaney's nose and nearly made her faint from hunger.

The server paused in her bustling from one table to the next. "Busy today. If you don't mind grabbing a couple of menus, you can take that corner table." She nodded in the direction of a table that still showed signs of recent bussing.

"Thanks." Delaney picked up the menus, and Devon indicated she should precede him. Despite his grumpiness and unapproachability, his manners were always impeccable.

Delaney tossed her bag onto the red vinyl bench and slid in, while Devon took the bench opposite her and studied the menu.

She didn't need to look—she'd have Ruby's chicken pot pie, and she'd enjoy every creamy, carb-filled bite.

Lisa, another waitress, walked past, a slice of chocolate cake the size of a microbus on her tray, and Delaney nearly whimpered.

"Would you like a slice of cake?" Devon asked. Her gaze shot to his face, and his eyebrows were lifted.

She shrugged. "Life's too short not to have dessert."

Mandy came to take their order. "Ladies first." Devon gestured to Delaney.

They placed their orders.

Circling back to the conversation, Delaney said, "I'll have you know, Dr. Mayfield, that I am gathering . . . *data* to prove to you and the committee that this is a viable degree. And I'm going to knock your socks off."

He lifted a brow. "Great." He sat back to allow Mandy to set their drinks on the table.

Taking a sip of her diet soda, she continued, "I'm going to take you and the committee to school and educate you on the romantic fiction market."

That got a grin out of him, a fleeting one, before he sobered, but it looked good on him.

"Looking forward to it."

**10**

―――――

Delaney dug into her chicken pot pie with gusto. It surprised him that he liked that she didn't fret over calories like so many other women. Her confidence in her curves made her even more enticing.

Setting her fork on her plate, she tilted her head. "So, how'd you end up in a small town in Northeast Georgia?"

"My story isn't very interesting." Especially since he had no intention of telling the whole thing.

"Come on." She reached across the table and nudged his arm. "We have to make polite conversation, otherwise it'll just be two people who happen to be eating at the same table."

"All right, I'll give you the condensed version. I grew up in Connecticut, attended boarding school, did my undergrad and master's at Harvard, then a Ph.D. at Wharton. Taught for a few years, became a department chair, then took the job at Sterling."

She snorted. "You haven't told me anything I couldn't find on your bio." Eyeing him, she took a bite of the pot pie, and his eyes honed in on her mouth as she licked some of the creamy sauce off her lips.

Smirking, she pointed at him with her glass. "Let me guess. Preppy, over-priced boarding school where you played Lacrosse, excelled at math and science courses . . ." She narrowed her eyes and tilted her head, as if studying him. "Class president and . . . oh!" She snapped her fingers. "Class valedictorian."

Damn. She was good. "Not bad, but not entirely correct. I played basketball."

"I could see that. Then what?"

He shrugged. "I earned an MBA from Harvard, before moving on to the Wharton School of Business where I earned a Ph.D. in Management with a specialization in strategy at the age of twenty-eight. I taught for seven years then became a department chair at the age of thirty-three, before accepting the position here."

"Quite the over-achiever." She propped her chin in her hand. "You don't strike me as an academician. Rather, I see you as the CEO of some multinational corporation, making a bajillion dollars, collecting your golden parachute before moving on to the next multinational corporation. Wash and repeat."

"Money's not an issue."

She lifted a brow. "Member of the Lucky Sperm Club? Do tell."

Wiping his mouth with his napkin, he took a sip of Ruby's sweet iced tea then gazed across the table into Delaney's sapphire-blue eyes, filled, to his surprise, with interest. He didn't mind talking about his business accomplishments. But 'family' was off limits.

"In undergrad, I started a company purely out of necessity. That personal necessity became an online textbook exchange for college students, where they could offer their used text books to other students in need of those same books. Sort of like an eBay for textbooks."

"I sold the company to the largest textbook supplier in the country for a tidy sum. The company figured college students were going to find a way to get their hands on discount textbooks, so why not profit from that too."

"Well, that explains the Tesla," Delaney muttered.

"Then, in grad school, I started another tech company, an idea that came to me as part of my master's thesis. The company was a web-based platform for bringing guest lecturers from around the world into classrooms, at a fraction of the cost to physically bring these same speakers in. The platform saved the schools from paying travel expenses, which for some of the heavy hitters, could break the bank, what with first class airfare, private cars, and hotel suites, in addition to a hefty honorarium."

He continued, "What started as a platform for the technical side of the guest lectures—things like satellite uplinks and video equipment—turned into a full-service company that handled the honorarium payments, the scheduling, and any materials needed for the lecture."

He slid his plate out of the way. "I later sold that company before earning my Ph.D. to an innovative education technology and services company for more zeroes and commas than I'd ever imagined possible."

"So, I repeat. Why academia?"

"I'm lucky. I can do whatever I want. And what I want to do is shape the minds of the world's future business leaders, and since I have more money than I could ever spend, I took what I learned both in the classroom, and in the real world, and became a professor at Wharton."

"You're an interesting man, Dr. Mayfield."

That simple statement from Delaney warmed him from the inside out.

"And a contradictory man." She tilted her head.

"How so?"

"You dress like you should be on Wall Street, yet you're a dean at a small university. You drive a Tesla yet live in a modest townhome in Georgetown Square. You are opposed to my proposal, yet you go out of your way to ensure that I have time to make my argument in its support."

"As I've said before, it's nothing personal. And it's only fair that you should be given the opportunity to defend your idea."

She pushed her plate aside.

"Are you having cake?"

"If you'll split it with me."

"Is it worth the extra mile I'll have to run tomorrow?"

"So worth it," she said with a wink.

"Let me guess, you walked."

"Of course. Why would I drive five blocks downtown to walk around an art festival?" They'd stepped out of the bright lights of Ruby's and into the falling dusk.

The festival vendors had packed up for the night, their tent flaps closed, and the crowds had thinned.

"We seem to be making a habit of this."

"What's that?" She turned to look up at him.

"Me escorting you home." He gazed down the street toward her apartment complex, hands in his pockets, as if disinterested.

"You really–"

"Don't have to?" The corner of his mouth lifted. "I know. But I'm going to regardless." Placing his hand low on her back, he guided her around the sign advertising Ruby's specials then walked beside her.

The air had cooled with the setting sun. A star winked on in the cloudless sky. They strolled along, Devon in no apparent hurry to ditch her at her door. They strolled in silence, but a comfortable one. Maybe they'd actually succeeded in establishing a truce of sorts.

She'd had a surprisingly nice time, and in some ways, this non-date felt . . . like a date. One of the better ones she'd had in recent memory, at that.

Devon was smart, he had impeccable manners, and he treated her with respect—something she hadn't experienced from a man in a very long time, unless she counted Nash and Ethan. Grudgingly, of course, she had to admit that maybe his opposition to her proposal wasn't personal.

They'd arrived at her door, and she turned to Devon. "Thank you. I know this may shock you to hear me say it, but you're not so bad."

He shook his head with a brief chuckle that she felt down to her toes. "I'll take that as a compliment. You're not so bad yourself." Then his demeanor changed. Not the serious, broody demeanor she'd grown accustomed to, but something intense and yet a little uncertain. "In fact," he stepped closer to her. "I'd like to kiss you."

"Oh," she replied on an exhale. In her experience, men didn't ask. They just assumed. Then took. "I, I think I would like that." Her knees quivered as his gaze dropped to her mouth.

Cupping her face, he closed the distance between them until they were only a breath apart and the air around them hummed with electricity. Instead of 'the love test,' Sam should call it 'the lust test,' because there was definitely a lot of *that* between him and Delaney right now.

He bent forward and put his mouth on hers, tentative at first, gauging her response.

*Ho-ly hell.* Her lips parted, and his tongue tangled with hers, and a throaty moan escaped—he had no idea whose.

*Spicy sweet.*

One hand curled into his shirt, then her purse and shopping bag hit the ground, landing on his foot, as her other hand wrapped around his neck.

The kiss exploded, going from a mere flame to a blazing inferno in seconds.

Delaney pressed her body against his, and he groaned in both pleasure and agony. His hands skimmed up her rib cage until they encountered those voluptuous breasts. He'd dreamed about her breasts. Then again, what red-blooded male wouldn't have? Her hardened nipples bore into his chest, and he took command of the kiss, backing her up against the brick wall of her apartment building.

A car horn blared as someone peeled out, bringing them to their senses, and they broke apart.

Wide blue eyes, filled with confusion, stared at him in search of answers.

He had none to give. He bent to pick up her purse and shopping bag and handed them to her. "I hope that wasn't fragile."

She just shook her head.

"Goodnight, Delaney."

Hands to her lips, Delaney shut the front door behind her and leaned against it for support. That had come out of the blue. Of course, she'd felt the sexual tension all evening, but she hadn't realized the feeling was mutual. And who knew the buttoned-up Dr. Devon Mayfield could kiss like that?

A kiss she had felt all the way down to her toes.

A kiss that could never, ever happen again.

*Ever.*

More's the pity, since that kiss had rocked her world.

Since the day she'd introduced herself in McGinty's, she'd wanted to push Dr. Mayfield outside the bounds of his control. And she'd succeeded. In a big way.

Pushing off the door, she wandered through her apartment in a hot-kiss-induced daze. Through the kitchen, skimming her hand across the countertops, into the dining room, around the table, along the hallway to her bedroom. Her lonely bedroom.

It had been far too long since she'd wanted someone like she wanted Devon Mayfield. Was it because he posed such a challenge with his polished manners and his impeccable dress?

She groaned. Why did she fall for the emotionally unavailable men? The men who looked hot as hell on the outside but were cold as ice on the inside?

Collapsing onto her bed, she remembered the feel of his mouth on hers. But *was* Devon cold as ice on the inside? Or did his reserved demeanor camouflage a passion lurking just beneath the surface of that implacable façade?

No man could kiss like that and be cold.

Flopping onto her back, she stared up at the ceiling.

This. Was. Not. Happening.

She was not crushing on a man who held the future of

her life's work in his hands. A man who would likely never support her proposal.

A man who'd kissed her like he never wanted to let her go.

Yeah. This was so happening.

**11**

———

On Monday, Delaney entered the creative writing department's main office to check her mail. As she sorted through the junk mail, academic journals, and invitations for speaking opportunities, Carolyn, the department's receptionist, walked by.

"Oh, Delaney. I was going to email you. You have a package." She moved behind her desk and lifted a sizeable brown paper-wrapped package.

*What could that be?* She hadn't ordered anything.

"A good-looking guy dropped it off. He your boyfriend?"

Delaney ignored the question.

"He left a card. I taped it to the package."

Curiosity aroused, Delaney accepted the parcel. "Thanks."

"Aren't you going to open it?"

*Not here.* Carolyn had a reputation as a gossiper, and Delaney had no intention of providing fodder for the gossip mill. "Later. I'm late for a meeting."

Carolyn released a disappointed sigh, and Delaney beat a hasty retreat to the relative privacy of her office.

She placed the package on top of her desk and stared at it, hands on her hips. Biting her lip, she reached for the envelope taped to the front, grateful to see the seal had not been broken by Miss Meddlesome.

She opened the envelope and pulled out a mono-grammed card with the initials DWM. Scrawled in bold masculine script:

CONSIDER THIS A FURTHER EXTENSION OF THE OLIVE BRANCH.
DEVON

Surprised by his gesture, she set aside the card and tore into the paper. Surprise turned to shock when she discovered the framed *Pride and Prejudice* poster she'd coveted at the art festival.

She dropped into the guest chair in front of her desk, hand to her mouth. He kept her constantly off balance. Every time she pegged him as the biggest jerk in the world, he did something nice.

And after spending Saturday with him, and that kiss at her door, she'd begun to think his jerkiness wasn't inten-tional. That maybe there was a reason for his Darcy-like broodiness, and it wasn't just arrogance or condescension.

"Hey Del, wanna join us for lunch?" Shelby said, as she walked into Delaney's office with Sam right behind her.

"What's this?" Sam leaned over the poster to get a better look. "Nice. It's perfect for your office."

"Did you get that at the art festival we missed?" Shelby asked, joining Sam in her examination of the artwork.

"Um, no."

"Your mom send it you?" Sam turned to her with a ques-tioning look.

"Guess again." Shelby picked up the card and handed it to Sam.

Sam gazed down at the card then up at Delaney. "Devon? As in Devon Mayfield, hater of romantic fiction?"

"That would be the one," Delaney mumbled.

"Huh. Maybe he wants to make amends." Shelby took the card and returned it to Delaney's desk. "Or maybe he wants to get in your pants," she continued on a laugh.

"Shelby." Sam placed her hand on Delaney's shoulder. "Or maybe he's come to the conclusion that my test is right."

Delaney's head snapped up. That couldn't be it. Could it?

"Oh, that's right! You two matched!" Shelby sat on the corner of the desk, crossing her khaki-clad legs.

"Love and hate are but two sides of the same coin," Sam pressed. "There's definitely a lot of chemistry between you two."

"I'll say." Shelby examined her nails. "That night at the play I thought I might need a fire extinguisher in case you two spontaneously combusted."

Delaney snorted and folded her arms across her chest. "The only reason we would have spontaneously combusted *that* night was from extreme annoyance." Now, *Saturday* night. Well, that was a different story. A fire extinguisher might have come in handy. Or maybe a fire *hose*.

Uncomfortable with this line of conversation, Delaney sought to change the subject. "Seriously, why do you think he bought this for me?"

"I don't know. Why don't you ask him," Shelby said, looking over Delaney's shoulder.

"He's standing behind me, isn't he?"

"Yup." Rising, she said, "Oh, is that the time? Sam, don't you have a meeting to go to?"

"You're making your getaway is what you're doing."

"Retreat is the better part of valor." And with that, Shelby and Sam high-tailed it out of her office.

"Ladies." Devon nodded then leaned on the door jamb, hands in his pockets as he waited for Sam and Shelby to leave. "I see you got the poster." Damn, he looked good enough to eat in a pearl-gray suit and charcoal tie. But, he needed to add some color to his wardrobe. He dressed so conservatively.

Delaney stood then started fidgeting with the paper the artist used to wrap the print. "Yes." She kept her back to him as she put the card back in the envelope.

"Don't you like it?"

She finally faced him. "I love it. You knew I would. It's just," her voice trailed off.

He pushed off the door jamb and stepped into her office, making it feel small and . . . steamy.

"It's just what?" His gaze captured hers and held.

"You shouldn't have."

"You liked it. I wanted you to have it. Nothing more."

"And Saturday night?"

He frowned and rubbed his chin. "Yeah. That was more."

"I don't know how I'm supposed to feel about that. And this." She pointed to the poster.

"Then you've got company."

His response surprised her. He always seemed so sure of everything.

She shook her head. "I don't know what to say."

"How about 'thank you'?"

"For the kiss or the poster?"

"The poster." The corner of his mouth lifted. "But, I should say thank you for the kiss." His eyes locked on her mouth, and she resisted the urge to lick her lips.

Her heart stuttered. She'd never been thanked for a kiss, and it was, well, sweet.

"If you have a hammer and nail, I can hang it for you."

Again . . . surprise!

"Uh, sure." Delaney walked over to the filing cabinet against the wall and, opening a drawer, pulled out the hammer. She had to rummage a bit for a nail. "Will this do?"

Devon had removed his suit jacket and laid it over the arm of her guest chair. Taking the nail from her, his fingers touched hers and she'd have sworn she'd felt a spark.

His eyes shot to her face, revealing that he'd had a similar reaction. "Yes. Now where would you like it?"

"On that wall." She pointed to the wall behind her guest chairs.

Devon stepped back, gauging the center of the wall. "Hand me the poster."

Delaney brought him the poster, careful not to touch his hands when she transferred it to him.

Holding it up, he asked, "How's this height?"

"Down and to the right just a little. Perfect."

He marked the spot with the nail. "Take this," he said, referring to the poster.

In order to do that, she'd have to reach across his body. She bit her lip, hesitating.

"Delaney?"

Taking a deep breath, she moved in, reaching up. Her breast brushed his arm for a second, and they both froze.

Clutching the poster like a life raft, she backed away,

avoiding his gaze, while he focused his attention on hammering the nail into the wall, using a tad more force then seemed necessary.

She leaned the poster against the chair, so she wouldn't have to hand it back to him, and under the guise of checking the positioning, walked behind her desk. Rather than studying the poster, she studied Devon's broad shoulders and tight ass as he stretched to hang the picture. He wore suits more often than not, but he wore them so well.

She tilted her head in admiration.

"How's that?"

"Huh?"

"Is it straight?"

She blinked, refocusing on the cover of *Pride and Prejudice* that now hung on her wall. "Oh. Yeah. Perfect."

He stepped back, examined his handiwork, then handed her the hammer, careful not to touch her this time.

"So, what now?"

"What do you mean?" he asked with a frown.

"We've kissed. You gave me a gift. You hung said gift. Have we declared a ceasefire? Signed a peace treaty? What?"

"Depends."

"On what?"

"On you."

"I don't follow."

"For my part, I'd say we've signed a peace treaty, but if I vote against your proposal again, I fear another declaration of war."

She crossed her arms over her chest and narrowed her eyes at him. "You won't. Because the presentation I have is going to knock your socks off."

He pulled his jacket back on, buttoned it, then adjusted

the sleeves. "So you've said. We'll see." As he walked out, he cast a glance over his shoulder, an uncharacteristic grin on his face.

Annnd the jerk was back.

**12**

———

Why had he come? Oh yeah, because Ethan, who had become a valued friend, had invited him. *Friend.* A first for him.

Devon stood in an out-of-the-way corner, scotch in hand, watching the festivities. Sam and Ethan wandered through the crowd hand-in-hand, greeting guests and accepting congratulations.

Sam made a beautiful bride, but she wasn't the woman who'd caught his attention the moment she walked down the flower-strewn aisle. No, it had been a curvy blonde in peach silk. She wore her hair up in some elaborate twist, tendrils curled around her face and along her neck. She resembled a character out of some Jane Austen novel. But she was far too sexy for the proper manners of Regency England. And what he wanted to do with her probably wouldn't have been considered Regency appropriate either.

Scanning the reception tent, his gaze landed on the object of his fantasies. She had a smile for the elderly gentleman talking with her. She often wore a smile, and he found himself looking forward to seeing it. Then he recalled how that mouth tasted, the scent of her perfume, the feel of her pressed against him. Maybe her smile wasn't the only thing he looked forward to.

Shaking his head at the nonsense of the thought, he sighed, wondering how long before he could politely exit the love fest.

He nodded at Nash and Shelby as they walked by. He'd never felt so out of place, but with his newfound friends in pairs, he often felt like the fifth wheel. He gathered Delaney felt the same way.

Maybe they could do something about that.

AS THE BRIDE and groom made their way to the dance floor for their first dance as Mr. Dr. and Mrs. Dr. Quinn, a familiar sense of longing washed over Delaney. With a *soupçon* of jealousy.

She was so happy for Ethan and Sam. They made an amazing couple, inside and out.

But.

Her heart ached a little too.

The wedding tent on the grounds of the quaint white country church was decked out with white fairy lights, cream-colored linens, centerpieces of peach peonies, white roses, and dusty miller. Beautiful. Elegant. Understated. Just like Sam.

Scanning the room for someone to talk to, her gaze landed on Devon, standing by a potted palm near the bar, one hand in the pocket of his suit trousers, the other holding a drink. Looking uncomfortable with the festivities.

She hadn't seen him since he'd hung the poster in her office.

A glass of wine sounded good, so she turned her steps in that direction just as "All of Me" morphed into "Shut Up and Dance," and the wedding guests applauded the bride and groom.

Waiting her turn at the bar, she glanced over at Devon. The Widow May Carpenter, Sterling's last living debutante, had him cornered, probably telling him all about her latest brush with death. According to May, she'd been near death for about five years now. Yet, when they called for the single ladies to make a grab for the bridal bouquet, she was always there hoping for another chance at love.

Delaney couldn't fault her for that. If only she could have a *first* chance at love.

After ordering a sauvignon blanc, she took pity on Devon and joined the conversation. "Mrs. Carpenter! You're looking lovely in lavender."

"Oh, Delaney! This old thing? It's at least a decade or two old," she said, a blush tinging her leathery cheeks. She was ninety if she was a day.

"Well, on you it looks fresh as a daisy."

Mrs. Carpenter patted her on the cheek. "Thank you, dear." Then she scanned the room, on the hunt for fresh meat. Finding her prey in the form of Mr. Greybow, the officiant, she made her way through the crowd.

"Thank you," Devon said, acknowledging Delaney's good deed.

"You're welcome." She raised her glass to her lips. "Now you owe me," she joked, sending a flirtatious smile his way, just to see if she could shake that cool-as-a-cucumber demeanor.

"Oh, is that the way it is?"

"Yes. And I know the perfect way for you to repay your debt."

"Vote to approve your new major?"

"Well, that too. But I was thinking of something more immediate. And perhaps less painful for you."

Setting her drink aside, she plucked his from his hand and set them both on an empty tray behind them.

"Hey," he protested.

Taking his hand, she pulled him toward the dance floor.

"Oh, no." He dug in his heels. "I don't like to dance."

Dropping his hand, she spun to face him, hands on her hips. "What do you mean you don't like to dance? Everyone likes to dance."

"No, they don't."

"You mean you *can't* dance."

"No. I can dance. I just don't like to."

"Well, get over it." She grabbed his arm and tugged, thinking he was going to stand his ground and not budge. Instead, he reluctantly followed her out to the dance floor.

"Let's bust a move," Delaney said when they found an open spot.

Before she could get in her first hip waggle, the song changed from fast to slow. Stifling a groan, she turned to him with a sheepish expression. It was one thing to ask Devon to shake his groove thing. It was another thing entirely to get up close and personal in a slow dance.

Memories of The Kiss flooded her with warmth and want.

Just as she'd been about to let him off the hook, his hand encircled her waist and reeled her in.

"Where do you think you're going?" Devon asked, his broad hand warm and firm on her back, his other hand clasping hers.

～

"You don't . . . I mean, we don't–"

"Relax. You dragged me out here, now let's see this thing through."

Delaney's luscious curves fit him to a T. The smell of her perfume tickled his nose and sent heat straight to his groin.

He'd been watching her all evening, from the moment she walked down the aisle in her bridesmaids dress the color of the ripe peaches Georgia was famous for. He'd watched her flirt with the elderly Dr. Vanderkirk, a former dean of the College of Business. She'd brought a very pregnant Kara Blakely, wife of the mathematics department chair, what looked to be a glass of cranberry juice. She'd made a lonely old woman feel beautiful, and saved him in the process.

Everywhere she went, she brought sunshine.

And he'd come to realize his life could use a little sunshine.

Delaney was the slab of cherry pie topped with whipped cream that you shouldn't be eating. The wife he'd had in mind was the celery stick you *should* be eating instead.

After a few turns, Delaney sighed and relaxed into him. And damn, if it didn't feel good. Too good. He remembered how she felt pressed against him, her lips soft, warm, and willing under his. And he wanted more. So much more.

The truth was, she scared him. Made him feel things he'd never felt for anyone before. Things like compassion, warmth, and caring—things that made him weak and vulnerable, made him need and opened him up to rejection. Not a position he relished. Maybe if he'd grown up with a nurturing mom or a supportive father, those feelings wouldn't seem so alien to him now.

Her free hand slid up his spine and back down and his

knees nearly buckled. The hand he clasped in his gave a slight squeeze.

Before he could consider it, he pressed his lips to her temple, and she sighed, shifting his thoughts to making her sigh for other, more erotic reasons. Wondering how she would sound as he kissed and nipped his way down that voluptuous body of hers.

*Damn.* If he didn't put a stop to this fantasy, he'd be hard-pressed—no pun intended—to exit the dance floor without alerting Delaney and everyone else to his predicament.

Then she turned her mouth into his neck, and her hot breath against his skin solidified his growing erection.

*Sweet Jesus.*

The way she was pressed up against him, she had to feel what she was doing to him.

The song ended, and Delaney took a step back. His undoing came when she glanced at his crotch, licked her lips, and raised her wide-eyed gaze to his. The air crackled with so much electricity he expected all the wedding guests to spontaneously combust.

"Thank you for the dance, Devon."

And then she was gone.

*Way to go, Devon.* Now she thinks you're not only an asshole, but a horny teenager.

DELANEY TOSSED the peach-and white-rose bridal bouquet onto the dresser as she stepped out of her stilettos. If she had a dime for every wedding bouquet she'd caught in the last two years, she could pay off her car and take a vacation to Hawaii.

Slipping off the full-length chiffon bridesmaid's dress, she reached into her closet and pulled out her fluffy white robe. She needed the comfort and assurance the robe offered. Belting it, she sank onto the bed behind her and began taking the pins out of her hair.

Earlier, on the dance floor with Devon, when she'd felt his lips on her temple, followed by that unmistakable bulge, she'd come close to grabbing his hand and hauling him off to some secluded spot outside the wedding tent for a hot, quick romp. The thought of making Devon Mayfield lose control, and in a public place, made her shiver in anticipation.

Then common sense took hold. *Thank God.*

Sex with Devon was a bad idea. The worst. Even if Sam's test said they were a match. And even though his kiss was the greatest thing since milk chocolate . . .

Not only were they at odds over her proposal, if she fell for him and his broodiness, she'd never forgive herself. After a failed six-month relationship two years ago, she'd sworn off her Kryptonite—emotionally unavailable men.

If she wanted a serious relationship, Devon Mayfield was *not* the man. She wasn't Elizabeth Bennet, and he wasn't Fitzwilliam Darcy.

She thought about what Shelby had said. *Stop trying so hard.*

That's what she intended to do. Focus on her career, and give Mr. Tall, Dark, and Brooding a wide berth. The only contact she planned to have with him was during the curriculum approval process. No more bumping and grinding on the dance floor, no more dinners at Ruby's or picnic dinners on The Green. Or hot kisses outside her front door.

Devon Mayfield was off her to-do list.

Her mind made up, she decided a long, hot bath was in order. Maybe it would calm the sexual frustration she'd been feeling since their slow dance together. Who was she kidding? Since The Kiss.

A few candles, a glass of wine, maybe a chocolate or two, and she'd be right as rain.

Mostly.

Flipping on the bathtub faucet, she dug around in the cabinet for bath salts and candles. Coming up with lavender bath salts and a couple of vanilla candles, she set the scene. While the bathtub filled with hot water and the bathroom filled with the scents of lavender and vanilla, she headed to the kitchen and the open bottle of chardonnay in the fridge. Holding it up to the light, she saw it was more than half full. Perfect.

Uncorking it, she poured a glass then hurried to check the water level.

A quick sip, and then she set the glass on the edge of the tub. Twisting up her hair, she secured it with a clip and shucked her robe.

Easing into the hot water, she sighed. Leaning back, she clasped the wine glass, closed her eyes, and . . .

The doorbell rang.

"Oh, come on! You can't be serious." Who the hell could that be?

It was only about nine-thirty, so it wasn't late. It could be her neighbor, Jenny Stevens, whose husband was currently overseas serving his country.

"Oh God. What if it's bad news?"

Climbing out of the tub, she wrapped her robe around her, not even bothering to dry off. Just in case, she grabbed the baseball bat she kept by her bed.

She reached the door and peered through the peephole.

And there stood Mr. TD&B himself. Looking über hot in his suit pants, *sans* jacket and tie, sleeves rolled up over his forearms, his white shirt open at the neck.

Did he come to finish what they'd started? Her resolve began to crumble like dry cornbread.

Chewing on her lip, her hand poised at the deadbolt, she debated with herself. Should she open it? It was clear she was home. The lights were on in the living room and the kitchen. He could think she was in the shower—or bath—which, technically, she had been.

But.

Maybe something was wrong. She peeked again. He did have a frown on his face. But then again, when didn't he?

Compassion won out over common sense and she opened the door.

"Devon. What's wrong? Why are you here?"

He gave her a sheepish look. "I, uh, I came to apologize."

**13**

———

This had been a mistake. A colossal mistake.

Clearly Delaney had been in the shower. Or the bath.

Devon scrubbed his hands over his face attempting to wipe the vision of Delaney, her body slick with water and suds, from his imagination. He nearly groaned aloud.

Her hair hung in damp ringlets along her neck, and her wet robe clung to her curves, especially her breasts, free and unhindered by a bra, their nipples pebbled against the fabric. He knew those breasts would feel heavy in his hands. The scent of lavender assaulted him.

"Apologize? For what?"

He cleared his throat. *Get it together, man. Or you'll be apologizing for much more than your behavior on the dance floor.*

"For my inappropriate behavior on the dance floor, and even more for my . . . reaction."

Her brow puckered, whether in anger, or just in thought, he couldn't tell. Then she cinched the tie on her robe tighter, folded her arms across her chest, boosting her breasts even higher. He was making her uncomfortable. Again. Which was not his intention.

"It's okay." She looked up at him with those breathtaking baby blues.

The silence grew as the tension went from a five to a ten on the Richter scale. *Speak, man! Say* something, *anything.*

"Well, I'd better go, and let you get back to your . . ." He waved his hand in the general direction of her damp hair and robe. The robe that clung to her breasts like cellophane to a ripe melon. He swallowed hard. "Bath."

He turned to go.

"Devon?"

*Damn. So close.* "Yeah?"

"Did you really, um, want me tonight?"

This time he did groan out loud. He took a deep breath and responded. "Yes."

She nodded her head.

*That's it?*

As she put her hand on the door to close it, she looked him in the eye and said, "Ditto."

The door closed with a soft click, yet the honesty of her answer left him so stunned he couldn't move.

Delaney Driscoll was proving to be the most interesting woman he'd ever met. And the most frustrating.

Adjusting himself with a wince, he headed down the sidewalk to his car unable to get the vision of a naked and willing Delaney off his mind. He'd just reached the parking lot when Delaney's door opened again. He turned at the hopeful sound to see her silhouetted by the light, and damn if his mouth didn't water.

"Do you still? Want me, I mean?"

*Oh God, yes!* "Delaney." He'd intended for her name to

come out as a warning, and instead it came out gruff and wanting.

"Do you?" she asked again.

He closed his eyes. God help him. "Yes." When he opened his eyes, she held out her hand to him and opened the door wider.

*Sweet Jesus.* If there was a hell, he was going straight there. But by God, he would enjoy every minute of the reason for that trip.

DEVON HESITATED, and Delaney gave herself a mental forehead slap. *What was she thinking?* This had disaster written all over it. In ALL CAPS. Then he was on the move, stopping just short of her personal space. His eyes burned hot as his gaze captured hers.

Oh, what the hell. She was never very good at keeping to-do lists anyway.

Stepping into her, he reached back and closed the door. She stared up at him, her throat dry, her heart threatening to tap dance out of her chest. Apparently his wasn't far behind, given the thudding of the pulse in his throat.

His big, warm hands settled on her waist, and his eyes honed in on her lips.

*Oh yes. Kiss me again. Please.*

He tilted her chin up and she closed her eyes.

"Are you sure about this?"

She opened her eyes and nodded, trying to read his mood. Then he bent his head and captured her lips with his. Wrapping her arms around his neck to keep from sliding to the floor, she opened her mouth to him. Their tongues tangled and groans escaped them both.

Adjusting the angle, he backed her up against the door, his hands gliding up her rib cage, just below her breasts, which yearned for his touch. He parted her legs with one of his own and ground into her, his impressive erection pressing against her belly.

*Sweet Lord!* It had been far too long. Her fingers curled into his thick hair, holding his mouth to hers.

But he withdrew, his breath coming in harsh pants. He stepped back, leaving her bereft. "I'm behaving no better than Curtis." He scrubbed a hand through his already-mussed hair. And Devon Mayfield with messy hair was a sight to see.

"There's one big difference."

"What's that?" he asked, confusion skittering across his face.

"I didn't want Curtis." She reached out for his waistband and gave a tug, drawing him back toward her.

*Damn.* Those big blue eyes held his as she nibbled on her lower lip. She let go of his belt and they stood, not touching, only an inch of space between them. Her breasts rising and falling with each raspy breath, her hands went to the belt of her robe, loosening the tie, and then she opened it and let it slide from her shoulders and onto the floor.

Speechless, Devon held his breath at the sight. Perfection.

Creamy skin, still rosy from the heat of her bath, begging to be touched. And her breasts far exceeded his imagination. Large, pink-tipped nipples beckoned for his mouth. He lifted his hands, covering her, and her head fell back against the door.

"Beautiful." Bending forward, he brought a nipple to his mouth, circling it with his tongue, taking pleasure in her throaty moan. He moved to her other breast as her breath came out in a velvety sigh.

Raining kisses up her neck, his teeth found her earlobe and nipped, drawing another moan from her.

He slid a hand down her belly until he reached her core, sliding a finger inside her. Her eyes closed as he stroked her, her breathy pants heating his cheek.

"Devon," she cried out. She grasped his shoulders like a woman on the edge, as her release hit her.

He continued to stroke her through the aftershocks, pressing kisses to her temple.

"Too many clothes," she finally muttered, as her eyelids fluttered open and her hands began working on the buttons of his shirt. She tugged it out of his pants and drew it off his shoulders.

The look on her face nearly brought him to his knees. Pure unadulterated lust. Her hands skimmed his chest on their way south. He groaned in anticipation of them reaching their destination and almost exploded when she cupped his erection through his slacks.

She glanced up at him from beneath her lashes, a saucy smile on her face. Damn, but everything about her screamed sex. And he was more than willing to oblige.

"Bedroom?" he rasped. "Where's your bedroom?"

Taking his hand, she led him through her apartment in all her naked glory. It could have been furnished in leather and fur for all he'd noticed. He had his eyes on Delaney's delicious derrière and beautiful legs, his mind already several steps ahead, imagining those legs wrapped around his waist as he drove into her.

When they'd reached the dimly lit bedroom, she

returned to finish the job she'd started and unbuckled his belt. Making quick work of it, she unbuttoned his waistband, tugged the zipper down, and plunged her hand into the opening. Her hot little hand made contact with his erection, and whatever doubts he'd had about this encounter vanished.

He grabbed her wrist and pulled her hand out of his pants. "Hold on, Delaney, or this will be over before we start."

Scooping her up, he laid her on the bed and gazed down at the sexiest body he'd ever seen. In his life. Ever.

A gift of voluptuous curves wrapped in smooth, silky skin, adorned by eyes so blue they rivaled the summer sky, a sultry mouth meant for kissing, and a wealth of blond hair. And at the center of all that beat the heart of a woman that captured his imagination in a way no other woman ever had.

Slipping out of his shoes and socks, he then pulled his slacks and boxer briefs off. Her eyes never left his, until she glanced down and licked her lips before her eyes flicked back up to his face.

He wanted to take all night to get to know every honeyed inch of her, but he was screaming for release. Crawling onto the bed, he covered her, and then froze. "Tell me you have condoms."

"Bedside drawer."

*Thank God.* Reaching for the drawer, his body gliding along hers, hot skin to hot skin, his hand actually shook as he pulled a foil packet out of the box. Rolling on the condom, he then settled himself between her thighs and pressed into her, watching her face for any sign of discomfort. He slid into her with a long slow move and stopped, gritting his teeth.

"What?" Delaney asked at his hesitation.

"You feel so damn good."

With that, she wrapped her legs around him. "So do you."

Before he could embarrass himself by coming too soon, he slid her lower beneath him so he towered over her, propping himself up on his forearms, and picked up the pace. Delaney matched him thrust for thrust, her throaty cries driving him toward his release. She cried out just as he exploded into a million pieces.

As his breath slowed its frantic rhythm, Devon knew it would be a long time, if ever, before he had sex that good again.

"Oh. My. God. I have never—that is to say–"

He rolled off her and propped himself up on an elbow and brushed the hair out of her face. "Spit it out, Delaney. You've never been one to mince words."

She ducked her head against his chest. "I've never . . . come . . . like that . . ."

He pulled back to gaze into her eyes. "Never?"

"Well, I mean I've had orgasms. Of course I've had orgasms." She waved her hand as if that was a given, especially since he'd given her one against her front door minutes earlier. "Just not, you know, during intercourse."

A grin split his face, and he kissed her forehead. "It's all in the angle."

Devon Mayfield grinning was like the sun emerging from behind a dark cloud. "The angle?"

"Yeah, and it just so happens I was a very good student of geometry."

"Well, props to your teacher."

He chuckled.

She blinked, stunned. Devon Mayfield—the man who could give Mr. Darcy a run for his money in the brooding department—actually laughed. Her heart rolled over, and a warning bell sounded in her head. *Don't do it, Delaney. Don't fall for him. He'll break your heart into a million and one pieces.*

Still basking in the glow of two orgasms, she ignored the bell.

Devon rose from the bed and headed for the bathroom. She pulled the covers over her and admired his mighty-fine backside. Who knew buttoned-up Dr. Mayfield looked like that under those designer suits.

When he came back to the bedroom, he had a towel around his waist. "I interrupted your bath."

She rolled to her side and propped her head in her hand. "I'm not complaining."

"Good to know."

"So, geometry." She lifted a brow.

He nodded. "Angles."

"Got any more talents you'd care to share with the class?"

"As a matter of fact, I do."

She threw the covers back, and with a flick of his hand the towel dropped to the floor.

"There's one in particular, but first things first." He crawled up the bed, settling between her legs and grinning up at her before putting his mouth on her.

"Oh God."

Maybe she'd underestimated the importance of geometry.

**14**

───────

After two rounds of the best sex he'd ever had, Devon's mind turned to the awkward post-sex dilemma. Should he stay or should he go?

His first inclination was to get up, get dressed, and get the hell out of Dodge. However, Delaney's warm, luscious curves pressed up against him, beckoned him to stay. The arm he had wrapped around her waist felt like lead. Indolent and sated, he could barely move, even if he'd wanted to.

"I smell smoke," Delaney muttered against his neck, where she was currently nestled. Her warm breath raised gooseflesh as he remembered the way her mouth felt on other parts of him.

*Jesus.* Twice in a row wasn't even enough.

"Smoke?"

"Yeah. You're thinking too hard."

He snorted. Right now, his brain was the only part of him functioning. But as she slid her leg along his, another part of his anatomy sprang to life.

"Don't make this a thing," she said, as she rose to her forearm and tucked her hair behind her ear. It was no use trying to tame her thoroughly sexed hair, but Delaney was a woman completely comfortable with her sexuality.

"A *thing*?"

"Yeah, you know, 'Do I leave or do I stay?'" She gazed down at him, and heaven help him, he craved her lips on his again. "It's okay. Whatever you feel comfortable with."

"Now there's a trap if I've ever heard one."

She sat up, dragging the sheet with her and covering those magnificent breasts. "Devon, I enjoy your company–"

He chuckled. "Company? Is that what they're calling it these days?"

She shook her head with a laugh. "But I understand if you feel the need to leave."

Who *was* this woman? She wasn't begging him to stay? He took in the smooth skin of her shoulders, the tumble of blond hair, the sapphire-blue eyes that gazed at him patiently waiting for his decision, and for some inexplicable reason, he wanted to know Delaney in more than just the biblical sense.

"Do you have any of that wine I saw in the glass beside the tub?"

She nodded.

"I'll take a glass."

Smiling, she rose from the bed, unashamed of her nakedness, and headed for the kitchen.

BY THE TIME Devon entered the kitchen, Delaney had pulled on her robe, opened the bottle of wine, and poured two glasses.

She took a sip of hers and handed him his. "Hungry?"

"Famished."

"I have some sliced Gouda, salami, and crackers. Oh, and a jar of Kalamata olives."

"An antipasto plate, then?"

She chuckled. "Of sorts."

Devon had on his suit pants, his shirt untucked, the cuffs rolled up, his feet bare, and she could've eaten him up instead. Sex on a stick was what the disheveled Devon Mayfield was.

"Can I help?"

"No. I've got it. We'll eat in the dining room." She pointed around the corner with her wine glass.

Devon took his glass and followed her direction.

She pulled the items out of the fridge then took a platter down from the cabinet above her and began arranging slices of cheese and salami on it. Then she grabbed the crackers from the pantry and scattered several alongside the toppings. Next, she opened the olives and put a few in a small bowl then set the bowl on the platter.

Rounding the corner into the dining room, she saw Devon standing in front of a bookcase holding a framed photo.

"Your mother?"

"Yes." She set the platter on the table and went back to the kitchen for some napkins and small plates.

When she returned, he'd placed the photo back on the shelf and picked up one of her and her mother, along with the man Delaney considered her grandfather.

At the sound of the plates touching the table, he turned. "Looks good."

"It might not be gourmet fare, but it'll do in a pinch."

They sat across from one another and dug in. Hot, steamy sex really worked up an appetite.

Devon popped an olive into his mouth then pointed at

the photo of her mother. "Tell me about her, this woman who cared for Eliot all those years while you were away."

He remembered her cat's name? *Aww.*

Around a mouthful of cracker topped with cheese and salami, Delaney said, "Well, Carly Driscoll is a trust-fund baby but was black-balled when she got pregnant with me outside of wedlock and then refused to name the father, much less marry him."

She sipped some wine, ate an olive, then continued. "So she packed up and took her trust fund and baby girl to Kansas—Wichita at first. Then she bought some land about fifty miles outside of town and built an artist commune."

She got an eyebrow lift out of him over that tidbit of information, but he didn't interrupt. "My mother loved art, of all kinds, not to mention the artists who created it. I'm certain my father was a starving artist."

"You don't know who your father is though?"

"Nope."

"And that doesn't bother you?"

"Not really." She propped her chin in her hand. "By the time I was seven, the artist commune had filled to capacity, so I had a large family. I never wanted for love or attention."

"You've never thought about trying to find him?"

"No. Why would I? What is there to be gained by it? It's not going to change who I am." She shrugged.

His brow furrowed at that statement, and she wondered if he thought she was being shortsighted, but before she could ask, he continued with his questioning.

"And your mom's family?"

"Never met them. Although I've seen photos of them in newspapers."

"How's that?" he asked, a look of confusion on his face.

She sighed and rolled her eyes. "My mom's family owns the privately-held Driscoll Luxury Hotel Chain."

Devon sat back in his chair. "Seriously?"

"Yeah, why? You know it?"

"Do I *know* it? It was one of the companies we studied in a course on privately and closely held corporations. They have award-winning hotels all over the world."

"That's them."

He shook his head. "How is it that your grandparents never met you?"

"I was a bastard child of some lowly artist. As far as they were concerned, they wrote me and my mother off the moment they learned I was conceived." She lifted a shoulder. "If it weren't for the fact that the trust fund was under the control of a private manager, they would have done their damnedest to take that from her too."

Swirling the wine in her glass, she continued, "I never felt like I missed out on anything. My mother is a bit flighty, but she always put me first."

"And school? Were you educated on the commune?"

"No. I attended a small private school that employed the Sudbury teaching method."

"Sudbury? I'm not familiar with it." He layered another cracker with smoky Gouda and salami then handed it to Delaney.

*Such a gentleman.* "Thanks."

Taking a bite, she chewed for a minute and washed it down with a sip of wine. "Under the Sudbury method, students have complete responsibility for their own education, and the school is run by a direct democracy in which students and staff have an equal vote. There was no set curriculum or courses, and students were not separated into age groups."

"And you actually *learned* something?" he asked, incredulous.

Poor Devon. She could understand his shock over that revelation.

"Oh, I thrived in the free-form environment. But college, with its structured curriculum and courses proved to be a shock." She lifted a shoulder. "I adjusted quickly, especially once I landed on my major—creative writing and literature."

He pointed at her with his wine glass. "Middlebury College, right?"

"Right. How'd you know that?"

He stopped chewing, as if he hadn't meant to blurt that out. "I looked up your bio the day I received your degree proposal."

"Huh." She let that percolate a moment. Devon Mayfield had checked her out.

"So, boarding school," she said, clearly remembering their conversation in Ruby's. "That explains why you're always so buttoned up."

"What do you mean?"

"Nothing but suits for work, I've never seen you in jeans, your hair is always perfect. You know, buttoned up. Unapproachable."

*Unapproachable?* That's the second time she'd used that word to describe him.

"If I'm so unapproachable, why did you *approach* me at McGinty's that day?"

"I needed another drink," she said with a hand wave and some chagrin.

"Uh huh," he replied, unconvinced that was the only reason.

She ran a finger around the rim of her glass. "True confession—I've always had a thing for unapproachable men. You know, the Mr. Darcys of the world." She lifted her gaze to his. "I want to see if I can ruffle their perfectly preened feathers."

"And you think you ruffled my feathers?" He dropped his gaze to her mouth.

"Yes." She licked her lips. "And tonight I loved watching you lose control."

Heat settled low in his belly at her bold statement. And damn if he didn't enjoy the hell out of losing control with her.

Delaney rose from her seat, pulling loose the ties of her robe, leaving it to hang open. Climbing onto his lap, she straddled him. "And I'm going to enjoy watching you lose control again." She plunged her fingers into his hair, as she claimed his mouth with hers.

Gliding his hands up her ribs and around to her breasts, he growled with pleasure. Yeah, he thought, as she plundered his mouth with her own. Turned out losing control with Delaney was the most enjoyable thing to happen to him in a long time.

Maybe ever.

DELANEY ROLLED over in bed and cracked open an eye. She felt well-used and thoroughly relaxed. Guess three rounds of sinful sex did that to a girl. Glancing over at the empty bed, she sighed in disappointment. Devon must have left at first light so he wouldn't have to do the walk of shame.

Then she smelled it—coffee. Bless him, at least he'd made coffee before he'd left.

Rising, she wrapped her robe around her and tied it then gathered her hair into a twist and secured it with a clip she'd tossed onto the bedside table. First coffee, then a shower. Then maybe she could face the repercussions of last night's amazing sexscapade.

Stumbling into the kitchen, in an oxytocin-induced haze, she grabbed a coffee mug and filled it to the rim. Then she spotted the note in handwriting she now recognized as Devon's.

DELANEY,

IT WAS NOT MY INTENTION TO SNEAK OUT, BUT I HAD A SESSION SCHEDULED WITH A PERSONAL TRAINER THIS MORNING, AND I DIDN'T WANT TO WAKE YOU.

I'LL CALL YOU LATER.

D

SHE COULDN'T SUPPRESS the teenage-like giggle. "He'll call me later."

Uh oh. If that didn't sound smitten, she didn't know what did.

**15**

––––––

few days later, Delaney, Sam, and Shelby gathered around the table in Shelby and Nash's kitchen to look at one another's candid wedding photos. The professional photos wouldn't be ready for another week.

Sam and Ethan would take their honeymoon next month—two weeks on the island of St. Lucia, after a conference where he was the keynote speaker.

*Wistful sigh.*

Salt-rimmed glasses stood at the ready for the pitcher of margaritas Shelby had whipped up. And to soak up the alcohol, a platter of munchies.

Shelby poured the drinks, as Sam reached into a tote bag and pulled out her iPad. "Before we start on the photos," Sam said, setting the tablet on the table and turning it on, "what's up with Devon?"

Delaney choked on her margarita.

Shelby and Sam glanced at Delaney then at each other.

"He still opposing your major?"

*Oh. Whew.* Sam wasn't asking, 'What's up with Devon?' as in 'What's going on with *her* and Devon?'

"Yeah."

Then Delaney felt Shelby's eyes on her. "Are you wearing new blush?"

*Uh oh.* "No."

"Lipstick?"

"No." Shifting uncomfortably in her chair, Delaney reached for a bacon-wrapped date, but Sam smacked her hand.

Delaney's gaze shot to Sam's face. "What?"

"Not until you spill."

"Spill what?"

Lifting her hand and indicating Delaney's face. "This."

Delaney caved under the pressure of Sam and Shelby's silent interrogation technique. "I slept with Devon."

It was Shelby's turn to choke.

Sam just stared at her, bug-eyed. "No way. You *hate* him."

Delaney lifted her shoulder in a chagrined shrug. "Hate is such a strong word," she muttered, swiping salt off the rim of her glass and sticking her finger in her mouth with a wry grin.

"Oh my God!" Shelby and Sam exclaimed at the same time.

Then Shelby leaned over the table and whispered, "How was it?" as if there was someone else there to overhear their conversation. In fact, Nash and Ethan were in Atlanta for a Braves baseball game.

*How was it?* How was she supposed to answer that? She tapped her finger against her lips, as if in thought. "It was . . . fucking fantastic!"

Sam and Shelby looked at one another again then burst out laughing.

"You go, girl!" Sam said, lifting her hand for a high-five.

Delaney slapped her hand. It felt good to have that off her chest. She'd been dying to talk to her best buds about this.

"Once?" Shelby asked.

"Definitely not." Delaney reached for the date she'd wanted earlier.

"Whoa! Then how many?"

Delaney began counting silently on her fingers before giving up. "You know me and math. But a lot."

"More than a couple?" Sam pressed.

Delaney nodded.

"More than several?" Shelby cajoled.

"Yeah, I'd say more than several." Delaney knew she was wearing a silly grin.

Shelby waggled her fingers. "Details. When? Where? How?"

"Shel, if you don't know the *how* yet, I'm deeply disappointed in Nash," Delaney said, and laughed.

Sam snorted and prodded Delaney to spill.

"Well, it was the night of your wedding."

Sam's eyes grew wide. "Seriously?"

"Yeah." Delaney told them about the sexy slow dance, about Devon coming over afterward to apologize, and how one thing led to another. "And let me tell you, if Devon Mayfield is hot perfectly coifed, he's beyond smokin' with bedhead." In fact, Devon Mayfield with bedhead and a satisfied smile is the hottest thing she'd ever seen.

"So what now?" Sam asked, a concerned expression on her face.

Good question. But Delaney didn't want to think beyond the great sex, so she shrugged. "We're just having fun."

Shelby glanced over at Sam then back at Delaney. "Honey, it's all fun and games until somebody's heart gets broke."

"Meaning mine," Delaney muttered. "I'm going into this with my eyes open." *Well, that sounded convincing.* "Look, I appreciate your concern, but–" she cut her eyes in Sam's direction, "test results notwithstanding, I have no illusions about Devon falling madly in love with me. We're just . . . I don't know, having fun."

"Yeah. You keep saying that," Sam pointed out.

"And by 'having fun' you mean 'having wild, uninhibited sex,' correct?" Shelby asked.

Delaney smiled and waggled her eyebrows. "Still waters run deep, if you know what I mean."

"Just . . . be careful." Shelby's gaze held nothing but support. "I don't want to show up at your apartment to find you listening to Taylor Swift singing about tears on her guitar."

Sam snorted. "Seriously. Or worse, bad blood."

Her friends knew her all too well.

SEVERAL DAYS after his sexual encounter with Delaney, Devon came to a stop at one of the town's few red lights, next to an electric-blue convertible Mini Cooper with the windows down and music blaring. He glanced over to see Delaney gyrating in her seat to some guy singing about 'funking you up.'

Why didn't the Mini Cooper surprise him?

She swung her head from side to side, that blond hair swirling around her, while tapping her hands to the beat on her steering wheel. Then she threw her head back and blurted out the lyrics, several notes shy of perfect pitch.

And he smiled. He couldn't help himself. Delaney inhaled life. And life, in turn, filled her up. He could take a lesson from her on that.

She finally looked over at him, momentarily froze, then laughed and waved as she hit the gas.

The car behind him beeped, and he realized the light had turned green.

The Mini Cooper turned into the Piggly Wiggly parking lot on the other side of the intersection.

As he drove past, he couldn't resist looking for her. Spotting that blond hair and that curvaceous derrière in snug jeans, he chuckled and shook his head. His car's collision-avoidance system activated, braking just inches from the bumper of the car that had stopped in front of him.

Gripping the steering wheel and taking a deep breath, he admonished himself, "Keep your eyes on the road, Mayfield, and off Delaney's delectable ass."

DELANEY'S PHONE CHIRPED, signaling an incoming text. Setting aside the student paper she was grading, she picked up her phone and smiled when she saw Devon's name.

COLLEGE MIXER TUESDAY NIGHT 7:00.

Biting her lip, she texted him back.

IS THAT A NEWS FLASH?

A few seconds later her phone chirped.

NO, THAT'S A DATE.

She snorted.

COCKY MUCH? I MAY HAVE PLANS.

The three dots appeared on her screen signaling that he was typing a response, and then another chirp.

AND IF I SAY PLEASE?

She rolled her eyes.

I'LL THINK ABOUT IT.

His reply came seconds later.

GOOD. I'LL PICK YOU UP AT 6:30.

"Pfft." She set her phone aside. She wouldn't even dignify that with a response.

They'd been sleeping together a few times a week, sometimes having breakfast together when he stayed the night. She enjoyed listening to the trials and tribulations of being a college dean, and he understood when she vented about a helicopter parent or gushed about a particularly bright student.

Initially, they'd seemed worlds apart, but in truth, they shared the same world and related to one another's experiences pretty well.

The one topic they didn't talk about was her degree proposal. The last thing she wanted was for Devon—or anyone else, for that matter—to think that she'd use sex to get what she wanted. So, with the curriculum committee meeting less than a week away, she continued to revisit and revise her presentation, and avoided raising the issue with Devon.

The other topic she was avoiding? What she would do if Devon voted against her proposal again.

Finished up with the last of the urgent emails, Devon sat back in his office chair, rubbing the ache in his neck. Too much computer work today. He should take a walk, work out the kinks from sitting too long, maybe walk over to Uncommon Grounds for some caffeine.

Who was he kidding? He only wanted to walk over to the coffee shop in the hopes of running into Delaney. He'd left her bed just this morning and he already missed her.

He smiled, recalling her car dance. Sexy, adorable, kind-hearted, smart Dr. Delaney Driscoll. What was that song she'd been dancing to?

Rising from his chair, he poked his head out of his office door to see if Rachel was at her desk. No sign. He returned to his computer and typed in a snippet of the lyrics blaring from Delaney's car speakers. Google came up with Bruno Mars' "Uptown Funk." That sounded about right.

Opening a streaming service, he typed in the name of the song and hit play when it came up. Catchy beat. He could see why Delaney couldn't sit still to it. He turned up the volume.

His foot tapping, his knee bouncing, he kept time with the rhythm. Unable to sit still, he stood up and moved his hips, fingers snapping. Chin bouncing, he did a little spin, bent his knees and bounced to the beat.

He'd had basic ballroom dance lessons as a reluctant teenager in boarding school. He could handle most social dance situations, from a waltz to a foxtrot, but this was . . . liberating. Swinging his head side to side mimicking Delaney, he spun around with a hip shake, arms over his head, and froze.

Leaning against the door frame, a cup of coffee in each hand, a gift bag dangling from her wrist, stood Delaney, a broad smile across her face.

She giggled. "Gotta love Bruno." She pushed away from the door and walked into his office.

He scratched his nose, as heat flooded his face. "How long have you been standing there?"

"Long enough."

He closed his eyes. *The one time he cuts loose, he's busted.*

"I loved it." She held out a coffee cup. "I thought you might need an afternoon pick-me-up. After all, we didn't get much sleep last night," she added with a wink.

No argument there.

Taking the proffered coffee, he walked around her, looked outside his door once again, then closed it behind him.

She lifted a brow. Standing there in a white skirt and a fitted blouse the color of her eyes, Delaney was the only afternoon pick-me-up he needed.

Lifting her hand, she said, "This is for you."

Setting his coffee aside, he took the bag. "It's not my birthday."

"I wouldn't know whether it was or not, since I don't know your birthday."

"It's next Tuesday."

"Really? We'll have to celebrate."

"Or not," he muttered. Pulling the pinstriped tissue from the bag—nice masculine touch—he peered inside to find a dress shirt. "Purple?"

"Yeah. To loosen up a little, put some color in your life. You can wear this with your pearl-gray suit and charcoal striped tie."

She patted his chest, but before she could remove her hand, he took it, and, moved beyond words, lifted it to his mouth and kissed it.

Gifts were an uncommon occurrence in his life. Carter sent obligatory gifts to the school every year for his birthday, usually practical items like laptop computers or tablets for his schoolwork. But those had stopped on his eighteenth birthday. Then there were the occasional gifts from co-workers, like when he moved on in his career, but nothing like this.

That Delaney took the time to pick out a shirt, considered what he should wear it with, and gift wrap it meant more to him that any other gift ever had.

The music changed to a slow song full of regret, and he plucked the coffee from her hand, setting it on the desk next to his, and took her into his arms. He began to sway to the music—as Bruno, was it?—sang about what he should have done when he had his girl. With his chin on her head, the scent of orange blossoms, the warm soft body pressed to his, he felt . . . content.

Delaney's hands skimmed along his back, easing the tension and removing all thoughts of faculty hirings, departmental budgets, and college rankings.

The song ended and Delaney withdrew, smiling up at him. He bent his head to kiss her. Just a quick peck—after all this was a place of employment—but a peck wasn't nearly enough. As his tongue grazed hers, she moaned and leaned into him, her hands going to his shoulders.

The kiss heated and, just as he considered bending her over his desk to see what she had under that flirty little skirt, she pulled back, her gaze cloudy with desire. Patting his chest, she said, "As much as I would like to take you up on that," she glanced down at his erection, "I have a class to teach in fifteen minutes."

Repressing a groan, yet thankful she had come to her senses before he did something altogether inappropriate, he nodded.

Her hand grazed across his chest as she retrieved her

coffee. "But, if you should find yourself in my neighborhood, say around sixish, I'll be home . . . trying on my latest Victoria's Secret purchase."

This time he did groan. "Lace?"

"*Lots* of lace," she said with a saucy wink.

He was a sucker for Delaney in lace. "I'll bring the wine."

**16**

As Devon stood talking to the chair of the management department, he kept an eye on Delaney as she circulated among faculty, staff, grad students, and administrators. The sapphire-blue dress matched her eyes and complimented her blond hair. It was conservative in cut, but nothing on Delaney would ever look anything but sexy.

She greeted students, faculty, and staff alike, with a radiant smile that made her eyes sparkle like the gemstones he often compared them to. Never met a stranger either. She knew what to say to break the ice and how to step away from a conversation without making the person feel slighted.

While she didn't have the polish he'd always thought he'd wanted in a wife and partner, she had something he'd come to value more—sincerity.

And she'd avoided any public displays of affection, lending credence to his introduction of her as a friend. A friend with closet benefits, since they had yet to go public with their . . . whatever this was.

But was that all she was? Did he want more? Did he

want to take her hand in public, wrap his arm around her waist and stake his claim to her, putting the rest of the men in the crowd on notice?

She approached him, a glass of wine in her hand. "I thought you might like something to drink."

"Thank you." He took a sip of the crisp, cold chardonnay. "Mm. I haven't had a chance to get something. Every time I head for the bar, someone stops me to talk."

"That's because you're the dean. Did I tell you how handsome you look in that purple shirt?"

"You like it? It was a gift."

"Well, someone has good taste," she said with a wink.

They looked up to see the provost, Dr. Chamberlain, moving in their direction.

"I'll just go get a bite."

"No. Stay." He wrapped an arm around her waist then leaned in to whisper in her ear, "I want you in my bed tonight."

DELANEY SHIVERED when Devon's warm breath caressed her ear, and then she heated at his remark. "Is it hot in here? Cause it feels hot in here to me."

He'd just staked his claim in a very public way.

Devon smiled at the provost. If it weren't for the heat in his eyes, Delaney would think he hadn't heard her.

"Dr. Chamberlain, you know Dr. Driscoll, professor of creative writing and literature?"

She didn't know what to make of Devon's PDA, in front of the provost no less. But she liked it. More than she should.

"Yes, Delaney. We met at the holiday party."

"Dr. Chamberlain," Delaney took his hand.

"Please, call me Ken." He patted Devon on the shoulder. "You're doing great work in your first hundred days, and I'd like to talk with you about another of the president's initiatives."

"Of course."

"Would you excuse me?" Delaney nodded at the provost as he dove into his topic. Devon's hand reluctantly slid from her waist, but the heat of his eyes on her as she walked away warmed her to her toes.

She could get used to this.

She'd never considered being in a relationship with another academic, having shared interests, shared lifestyles, and a depth of understanding between them about their daily lives that she wouldn't get with someone outside academia.

Maybe that's why they'd matched.

She wouldn't go there.

Regardless of that match, she held no illusions when it came to a long-term relationship with Devon. She'd enjoy it while it lasted.

And deal with the heartbreak that would surely follow when it ended.

"Are you going to do bad things to me?" she murmured against his lips.

"I'm going to do *very* bad things to you." He nipped her lower lip, as his thumb rubbed her hard nipple.

"Good." She sighed into his mouth.

"Keys," he murmured.

"Hmm?"

He stepped back. "Unless you want to give my neighbors a show, I need my keys."

"Oh. Right." She stepped back while he pulled his keys from his pants pocket.

No sooner did he have the door unlocked than he gave her a gentle shove into his townhome, where she promptly dropped her handbag to the floor and dove at him.

He caught her against him, his mouth claiming hers again, as he kicked the door shut behind them.

She'd ached for him all evening at the mixer, especially after she'd looked up several times to find his eyes on her. "Clothes," she panted.

"Don't care," he growled.

Backing her into the kitchen, lips against hers, he unbuckled his belt as he went. He stopped in front of an island. "Turn around," his voice a throaty snarl.

She complied, as a frisson ran down her spine.

"Bend over." He pulled her skirt up, baring her bottom. Sliding her panties down her legs, he steadied her as she stepped out of them. She gazed back over her shoulder to see him rip open a condom packet and roll it on, and she shivered in anticipation. He stepped up behind her and entered her in one smooth thrust.

The things he did to her—for her—were the stuff of every woman's fantasy.

His hand reached around her, stroking her body, and she gave herself over to him, promising her heart she could protect it, but knowing it was far too late for that.

Devon skimmed a hand over her smooth round ass, buried deep inside her, where it seemed he always longed to be.

Delaney Driscoll had spoiled him for every other woman. His plan to settle down with a proper wife no longer mattered.

She backed into him, her four-inch heels putting her at just the right height for him, and thoughts of proper wives and career plans evaporated.

He pulled almost all the way out before sliding back in. She let her head fall with a groan. "Devon."

"I've got you. Hang on."

She gripped the counter as he picked up the pace, driving harder and faster with every thrust. He reached around and resumed his stroking until he felt her tense then let go as she cried out with her release.

He followed her over with a mind-numbing orgasm.

As his breathing struggled to return to normal, he covered her back with kisses.

She reached around for his hand and gave it a squeeze, and the wall around his heart did something he never thought possible. It cracked.

Pulling out, he lifted her up and turned her to face him. Cupping her jaw, he studied her. "I didn't hurt you, did I?" He shook his head. "I'm s–"

"Don't you dare, Devon Mayfield." Her eyes flashed blue fire. "Don't you dare apologize for giving me the best sex of my life." As quickly as it ignited, the fire in her eyes extinguished, leaving a soft smolder behind, and she touched his cheek. "I love what you do to me. Don't hold back. Don't ever hold back."

God, she unraveled him. Made him feel things. Things that collided and merged, like lust and tenderness, hope and fear, want and need, until he didn't know which was which anymore. Gathering her close, he touched his lips to hers, softer, sweeter this time. The heat banked, for now.

"How about we take this to my bedroom where I can love you slow and easy this time?"

"I like the sound of that."

DEVON DRIFTED INTO CONSCIOUSNESS, wrapped around a warm, soft woman, his hand proprietarily cupping a perfect breast, and he felt . . . content. Satiated. Happy.

Interesting.

As he lay there listening to Delaney's even breathing, that happiness expanded into something . . . more. More with a capital "M."

When he took the time to think about it, the last few weeks had been some of the happiest. For the first time in his life, he had friends, good friends in Nash and Ethan, and even Sam and Shelby.

Delaney sighed in her sleep. And, not only did he have good friends, he had . . . what? What did he have with Delaney? Friends with benefits didn't seem to cover it. Fuck buddies—not one of his favorite terms—especially as it applied to Delaney, didn't seem to cover it either.

So, what was this? Extreme like? Intense fondness? Powerful affection?

One thing he knew it couldn't be—love.

He thought about Sam's test and the results. Could Sam be right? Were he and Delaney a perfect match?

Possibly.

But love didn't enter into it.

Devon Mayfield was not built for that emotion. It just wasn't in his DNA. Clearly, since he'd been abandoned first by one parent then rejected by another presumed parent.

But, even without love, couldn't he and Delaney form an

attachment to one another? Could she be the partner he'd been looking for? Would she be happy with a relationship that fell short of love?

He closed his eyes and let sleep overtake him, and dreamed of a life with Delaney.

DEVON KNOCKED on Delaney's door, a bottle of red in hand.

Shortly after, she opened the door, and he almost dropped said bottle of red. Dressed in a slinky black dress and black stilettos, her blond hair a tumble of waves, she took his breath away.

"Happy birthday!" She tossed colorful confetti all over him and her front stoop.

He laughed and shook his head. "I don't think I've ever been the recipient of birthday confetti before."

"Well then, it's high time." She took his hand and led him into the kitchen where delicious aromas reminded him that the sandwich he'd grabbed for lunch was long gone.

"I didn't know you cooked." He set the bottle of wine on the counter and pulled her in for a kiss.

She shrugged. "Not much. My mother says pick one thing and do it well. Pot roast is the one thing I do well in the kitchen."

He nuzzled her neck, eliciting a sexy gasp. "I can think of another thing you do well in the kitchen," he said, recalling a certain encounter of the hot kind in his kitchen that didn't involve food.

"Keep that up and dinner will have to wait."

"Promises, promises."

She patted his shoulder and he released her. "Wine?"

"Definitely."

As he uncorked the bottle, he watched her move around her little kitchen, admiring how her derrière looked in that black dress as she opened the oven door and bent over to check on the roast.

He opened a cabinet, found a couple of wine glasses, and poured the wine before spotting a bakery box from Sterling's local bakery, Sweet Tooth. Handing her the glass of wine, he nodded toward the box. "Is that what I think that is?"

A sly grin spread over her face as she lifted the glass to her lips. "Depends. What do you think it is?"

"A birthday cake?"

"Can't put anything past you, can I?" She walked over and lifted the lid to reveal a miniature chocolate confection for two decorated with the words 'Happy Birthday.'

Huh. Today he celebrated his thirty-fifth birthday, and in all those thirty-five years, no one had ever given him a birthday cake.

And damn, but that simple gesture touched him to the core.

"Thank you." Pulling Delaney in, he captured her mouth with his, tasting the dark fruit of the wine on her lips. She sighed then leaned into him, her curves pressed to the harder planes of his body, and his heart swelled.

He struggled to remember what his life was like before Delaney, and that scared the hell out of him.

Withdrawing, she lifted her gaze to his, her blue eyes warm. "I have something else for you."

"Tell me you're wearing black lace underneath that dress."

"You'll have to find out for yourself." She slapped a hand to his chest as he reached for her, determined to find out. "But that's not it."

He groaned and rolled his eyes. She slayed him with her brazen sexuality.

She went into the dining room and returned with a splashy birthday gift bag stuffed with colorful tissue and held it out to him with a flirtatious wink. He shook his head and took the bag from her.

Maybe it held something lacey for her to model. Not that she'd be wearing it for long . . .

He pulled the paper out of the bag, and in the bottom was a framed photo of the two of them at last week's BBQ at Nash and Shelby's house. Lifting the photo from the bag, his throat tight, he stared at the gift. Delaney sat on his lap, an arm draped around his shoulder, a big smile on her face.

But what surprised him most was the smile on his face. He looked . . . happy.

He had no photos, no mementos of Christmases past, no keepsakes from family vacations, nothing. Not even a photo of his mother.

Now he had this.

Beyond words, he wrapped an arm around Delaney's waist and vowed to show her how much this—and she—meant to him.

**17**

———

A few days later, Devon headed for his car in the faculty parking lot after a long day, looking forward to a glass of scotch, the latest John le Carré novel, and a quiet evening in.

Delaney and Sam were helping Shelby with wedding stuff—something about birdseed bags, whatever that was about. He'd see her later. He opened the back door of his car, tossed in his laptop case, then shut the door and turned around to find Nash and Ethan standing there, grins on their faces.

"A little birdy told us that you just had a birthday," Ethan said, clapping Devon on the shoulder.

*Delaney.*

"So, since the girls are busy with wedding things, we thought a boys' night out was in order," Nash added.

"Thanks, but that's not necessary." Devon waved them off.

Not taking no for an answer, Nash continued, "Of course it's not necessary. It's fun. And besides, that's what friends do."

"I'll drive." Ethan indicated his car parked across from Devon's.

Devon hesitated a moment, but in the face of their determination, he sighed and fell into line with Nash and Ethan. So much for a quiet evening at home.

Two hours later, Devon found himself at a trendy tapas bar in midtown Atlanta, a twelve-year-old scotch in his hand and the table loaded with plates of baby back ribs, tenderloin mac 'n' cheese, flatbread pizza, and something called pork cheek tacos.

Ethan raised his glass of scotch, and Nash followed suit with this beer. "To the birthday boy!"

"And a good excuse for ribs and beer," Nash added.

Devon lifted his glass in toast, ridiculously moved by Ethan and Nash's acceptance and camaraderie. They dug into the fare, content to eat in a comfortable silence until they'd taken the edge off their hunger. Then talk turned to their women and Nash's upcoming wedding.

"You nervous?" Ethan asked.

"Nah." Nash spooned more mac 'n' cheese onto his plate. "What do I have to be nervous about?"

"Second marriage and all that?" Ethan added.

"This is Shelby we're talking about. My best friend."

"Glad to hear it. I'd hate to have to kick your ass if you left her standing at the altar."

Nash snorted. "Not gonna happen. Not me leaving Shelby at the altar. And not you kicking my ass."

Devon could feel Ethan's eyes on him. He looked up while Ethan took a bite of ribs, chewed a minute, then washed it down with his drink. Pointing at Devon with the now-clean bone, he said, "You know, you've been awfully happy these last few weeks."

"Yeah," Nash nodded then wiped his mouth with his

napkin. "You've loosened up since we first met. You're more, I don't know … relaxed."

"Maybe it's the laid-back atmosphere of Sterling." *Or maybe it's all the scorching sex he'd been having lately.*

"Could be," Ethan said, helping himself to more of the flatbread pizza. "Or, it could be a pretty blonde with a sunny personality."

Nash glanced over at Ethan then back at Devon. "I'm going with the pretty blonde theory."

*Great.* Now they were going to talk about his … relationship … with Delaney. *Fine.*

"All right." Wary, he propped his elbows on the table. "You got me."

Ethan pointed his thumb at Nash. "What Dad's trying to say here is, what are your intentions with regard to our girl?"

*His intentions?* "Beg your pardon?"

Nash's gaze turned to Devon, making his shoulder blades itch. "Look, man. You're our friend. And so is Delaney." Nash leaned back in the booth.

"But?" Devon gestured with his scotch for Nash to continue.

"Don't be the guy," Ethan said instead.

"What guy?" Devon asked, afraid of the answer.

"The guy that rips out Delaney's heart." Ethan leaned over the table.

Devon took offense to Ethan's remark. He would never intentionally rip anyone's heart out, let alone Delaney's.

"I know you won't intentionally break her heart, but–" Nash said, before Devon could speak up in his own defense.

"But," Ethan interjected, "You could do it just the same."

"Delaney's heart is bigger and more open than anyone's I know. Don't be the guy that damages it," Nash said.

"Were you one of those guys?" Devon asked, pinning Nash with his gaze.

Nash looked away, a chagrinned expression on his face. "Uh, yep. Not intentionally. I did something stupid. Something I thought would help Shelby. Something I knew would piss her off and didn't tell her precisely because I knew it would piss her off. When that help got us both in hot water and I let it slip, there was hell to pay. And then I thought I'd lost her."

Devon directed his attention to Ethan. "And you?"

Ethan held up his hands. "No. In my case, it wasn't me. Let's just say mine is a tad hardheaded and it took a while to bring her around to my way of thinking."

"Just," Nash slapped a hand on the table to make his point, "don't be that guy."

So, if Devon broke Delaney's heart, his name would likely be mud around here, and he could lose the only real friends he'd ever had. And that included Delaney.

As she slathered cream cheese on her bagel, Delaney gazed across the glass and chrome breakfast table in Devon's townhouse. She'd been spending more time at his place the last few days.

He had a sexy case of bedhead, a shadow of stubble along his strong jaw, and a contented look on his face as he sipped his coffee and flipped through Sterling's humble local paper, the Sunday edition of *The New York Times* sitting at his elbow.

She'd certainly changed her tune these last few weeks. Gone from despising him for his refusal to support her degree proposal to loving him for his ability to challenge her. Make her work for what she wanted, fight for it even. And he'd made her a better person for it.

She paused with the bagel halfway to her mouth. *Whoa! Rewind the tape. Love?* Did she just admit to herself that she'd fallen in love with Devon? Taking a bite of the cinnamon raisin bagel, she pondered this latest turn of events.

Let's see, did she have all the signs?

Happiest when she was with him. *Check.*

Missed him when they were apart. *Check.*

Thought of him frequently throughout her day. *Check.*

Loved waking up with him, going to sleep with him, and sitting across the breakfast table from him. *Check, check, and check.*

Trembled at his touch. *Double check.*

And the biggie, do anything to make him happy. *Check.*

She sat back, chewed her bagel, and smiled. Maybe Sam's test was right. Maybe Devon *was* her perfect histocompatible mate after all. She'd just reached across the table to touch his arm when he picked up *The New York Times* and opened it to the front page.

"I love you, Devon."

All the color drained from his face, a stricken look as if he'd just learned someone had died, and her words hung in the air, either unwelcome or unheard.

"Devon? Devon, what's wrong?"

DEVON BLINKED, unable to believe the headline: BILLIONAIRE CARTER LIVINGSTON DEAD AT THE AGE OF 64.

He anxiously skimmed the story, picking up words and

phrases like 'cancer,' 'survived by' . . . 'three children, five grandchildren.'

Emotion clogged his throat. Anger? Resentment? Rejection?

But grief? No. Not grief. How could he mourn someone he'd never really known? Someone who'd never cared enough to know him?

He dropped the paper to the table like it had bitten him.

"Devon, please, tell me what's wrong." Delaney knelt by his chair, her blues eyes filled with concern.

And without thinking, he said, "My father died."

"What?"

She stood and picked up the paper, reading it, searching for a clue to what had sent his world spiraling out of control.

"I don't understand. Carter Livingston is your father?"

"Yes . . . No." He scrubbed a hand through his hair. "I don't know." Leaping from his chair, he paced the floor.

His own father had been sick, for months, according to the article, and he hadn't known. No one had bothered to get in touch with him. Collapsing on the sofa, he buried his face in his hands.

He'd always held out hope that one day Carter would contact him, would ask to meet him, would acknowledge Devon as his son. He didn't expect Christmas cards and birthday gifts, just recognition. Not for the money, or even for the name, but . . . because he was proud to call him son.

And now that would never happen.

He choked out a mirthless laugh. As if his little fairytale would have ever come true.

The sofa dipped, and Delaney's hand glided down his back in an attempt to soothe him, to assuage the hurt that could never be assuaged.

He'd always known he'd been unworthy of love. His

mother's. His presumed father's. Even Delaney's. And this turn of events confirmed it.

Love didn't exist in Devon's world.

He pulled away from Delaney, capturing her wrist. She'd been so patient, waiting for him to explain. But he couldn't. Not to her. Not to anyone.

Shame, bitterness, and isolation filled him.

"I can't do this," he said, his voice calm, quiet. He set her hand on her lap and released it.

"Okay. We don't have to talk about it right now–" Her understanding tore at him.

"No. I mean I can't do this at all." He forced himself to look into her eyes, eyes that held compassion and sorrow. "I can never give you what you need. What you deserve." His quiet, painful confession hurt more than he'd ever expected. "I can't love you. Ever."

Her eyes filled, first with pain, and then with tears.

She reached for him, but before she could touch him and crumble his resolve, he rose from the sofa and, turning, walked out the front door, closing it quietly behind him.

Yeah. He'd become that guy.

STUNNED, Delaney sat on the sofa, staring back at the front door.

What had just happened?

One minute she was telling him she loved him, and the next he'd walked out of his own house, leaving her. Rising, she crossed her arms, hugging herself, thinking that if she could just wrap up tight enough her heart wouldn't crash to the floor and shatter into a million pieces.

Vision blurred by tears, she saw the newspaper lying on

the table. Swiping away the tears, she walked over and picked up the paper to read the story that had so shaken Devon's world that he told her he could never love her, trying to piece things together. He'd said his father died, but his response hadn't been clear as to whether *this* Carter was his father.

"Livingston is survived by his wife, Melinda, his three children, Michael, Stuart, and Charlotte, and five grand-children..."

Devon wasn't listed.

She shook her head, a single teardrop splattering on the article.

Pressing a hand to her chest, where her heart thudded painfully with the weight of Devon's words, she couldn't help feeling sorry for the grown man whose little boy's heart had been broken today just as he had broken hers.

**18**

―――――

 week after Devon learned of Carter's death, and six lonely, hellish days later, Rachel knocked on his office door. "There's a Robert Stone here to see you."

Devon glanced up from the blank computer screen he'd been staring at for who knows how long. "Who?"

"He's says he's an attorney."

Attorney? His first inclination was to ask Rachel to tell him he wasn't in the market for an attorney, but a glimmer of . . . something gave him pause. "Send him in."

A short, stout man with thinning hair and glasses followed Rachel into Devon's office, his face dour. The man glanced around then stepped up to Devon's desk and reached out a hand. "Devon Mayfield? Thank you for seeing me without an appointment."

Devon shook his hand. "Have a seat."

"I don't have much time, as my return flight out of Atlanta is in four hours." He reached into his brief case and pulled out a sheaf of papers.

"I'm here on behalf of the Livingston estate."

Devon froze in the process of clearing a spot on his desk. "I beg your pardon?"

"Mr. Livingston left a bequest in your name." He cleared his throat. "The other family members were present at the reading of the will on Friday, but the family attorneys thought it best to meet with you alone."

"I'm sorry, but I don't follow." Devon's heart hammered in his chest.

"I'm sure you can understand the delicacy of the matter, what with Mrs. Livingston and the children ignorant of your existence." The gentleman placed the papers on the desk, facing Devon.

"What? How?" His breath left in a whoosh.

"I just need you to sign here, here, and here," he said, pointing to pages flagged with tabs. "If you'd like, you can fill out the paperwork for direct deposit of the bequest into the account of your choice," he continued, as he fished around in his brief case, before pulling out another form and placing it on top of the other papers.

Devon finally found his voice. "Mr. Stone, are you saying Carter Livingston left me something in his will?"

The attorney finally smiled. "I guess you could say that."

Delaney had drowned her sorrows for over a week, and while she knew getting over Devon would be a long time coming, it was time to get back to the business of life, even if that life had lost most of its joy. Shelby and Nash's wedding was less than a month away, and the last thing she wanted was to be the Eeyore of the group before such a happy event.

Her mother taught her to own her feelings, to wallow in her sorrow when it came, but then to move past it as best she could because life was too short to waste it feeling sorry for herself.

She tossed her sheets in the wash and turned it on. Her weeklong pity party had resulted in a pile of dirty laundry, an empty refrigerator, and a few extra pounds, which she'd have to lose in order to fit into her bridesmaid's dress.

Many times over the last week, she'd considered texting Devon, sending a sympathy card or flowers, but she had no clue what to say. She knew he was hurting, and as if it wasn't enough that she carried the burden of her own broken heart, she carried the burden of his broken heart as well.

From what she could piece together, Devon was either illegitimate and Carter Livingston never acknowledged him, or Carter never knew Devon existed.

Her plants near death, she turned her attention to watering and fertilizing them, even as her chest ached.

Delaney had noticed that Devon had no photos in his townhome, save the photo she'd given him for his birthday. His home otherwise lacked the typical memorabilia of life— birthday party photos, graduation photos, or even prom photos. There were no photos of his mom, his dad, or his siblings. It's as if he arrived on the planet all alone and lived the last thirty-five years that way.

Pausing mid-pour, the watering can fell from her fingers as she stifled a sob for the lonely child who no doubt believed himself unworthy of love and thus incapable of feeling that emotion for someone else.

But she knew better. She knew that if he allowed himself to, he could love. He just needed a nudge in the right direction. Or maybe a shove.

～

DEVON BRACED himself for Delaney's appearance. He'd been both dreading and anticipating this day since he'd walked out of his own home, leaving Delaney behind.

When he'd returned later that morning, Delaney was gone, as were some of the telltale signs of her involvement in his life. The one thing she'd left behind—the photo she'd given him for his birthday.

She walked into the conference room looking poised and professional. And beautiful, as always. The sapphire-blue dress she'd worn to his college mixer was paired with a black jacket and a single strand of pearls around her neck.

She didn't meet his gaze, instead greeting Dr. Gregors and handing him a thumb drive for her presentation.

God, he missed her. He'd barely slept in the last week and half, and when he did sleep he woke sweaty, entangled in the sheets. His life lost all color the moment he'd walked away from her. He had to fix it, he just didn't know how. How could he fix their relationship if he didn't even know how to love?

She stood at the front of the room, remote control in her hand, and, clearing her throat, glanced around the room, her eyes never meeting his.

Delaney didn't know who her father was and she didn't let that negatively impact her life. It was high time he got over himself. There's nothing he could do to change the past, but there was something he can do to change his *future*. For the better.

DELANEY ADVANCED to her last presentation slide, listing the various career options for her proposed degree, in addition to the obvious, which was romance author.

"While becoming a successful published romance author is the primary purpose of the degree, it also prepares graduates for positions in the lucrative romantic fiction market as editors and agents. I conducted a survey among twenty-five editors with the top five romantic fiction publishers." Delaney pointed to the fancy bar graph Shelby created for her. "The results showed their unequivocal support for hiring graduates with the proposed degree and for accepting interns in the program."

"Thank you, Dr. Driscoll," Dr. Gregors said, nodding. "That was a very informative presentation. I learned a great deal about the romantic fiction market and the career opportunities available."

Delaney heaved a sigh of relief and took a seat in the chairs along the wall reserved for guests. She had yet to make eye contact with Devon. As she'd scanned the committee members during her presentation, she always stared at a spot above his head. Cowardly, maybe, but she couldn't bear to look into his deep brown eyes, afraid she'd crumple into a heap of heartache.

"Let's open it up for discussion," the chair continued.

"I, for one, don't need any further discussion," Dr. Gordon said.

Delaney resisted an eye roll. The man reminded her of the Grinch. The only thing missing was the green skin. No wonder his ex-wife had cheated on him.

"I am opposed to approving a degree program for the writing and publication of smut about women of loose morals."

She sucked in a breath. Dr. Gordon had been a vocal critic of her proposal from the very beginning, but he'd never made it so personal.

Out of the corner of her eye, she saw Devon rise then

smack his hands on the table. "That's it." He glared at Dr. Gordon. "I'll ask you to keep this conversation civil. There is no cause to insult an entire genre of fiction simply because your late wife read it and you think that's why she had an affair."

A few snickers followed.

"I can assure you, there is likely another reason for her affair." Devon pointedly stared down Dr. Gordon, until he looked away with a *harrumph.*

"I do have concerns over the cost of the guest lecturers," Dr. Gregors interjected. "With travel expenses and honoraria, this is a pricey proposal. But I do think it adds to the interest and value of the curriculum."

As part of the new major, Delaney planned to invite guest lecturers to speak to students, including top romance writers, agents, and editors. Dr. Gregors was correct, the expense could be enormous, and while she'd applied for a grant from the National Endowment for the Arts, it wouldn't be nearly enough. She was actively seeking private funding, but no one had come through yet. Even the services of the company Devon had started and sold would cost her money she didn't have.

Devon sank back into his seat. "I know that I have been opposed to Dr. Driscoll's proposal. Unlike Dr. Gordon, my primary concern was the usefulness of the degree, whether it prepared our students to enter the work force with the tools they need to succeed, and whether there was a market for the degree."

Delaney held her breath. Although the newest member of the committee, Devon's opinion appeared to carry a lot of weight with the others.

He nodded at the screen and her last slide. "The data Dr. Driscoll has presented on the romantic fiction market, the top five publishers, as well as the smaller publishers that have emerged as a result of the impressive romantic fiction market share in the publishing industry, has changed my mind."

Delaney's throat clogged with tears. He caught her gaze, but his face remained an unreadable mask.

"I support the proposal to add a Bachelor of Fine Arts in Romantic Fiction and Literature. And I know a company that could help with the guest lecturers, greatly reducing the associated expense."

Delaney pressed a hand to her mouth to hold back a sob.

Even if the committee voted against her proposal in the end, Devon Mayfield had restored her faith, if not her heart.

**19**

---

"**D**evon!"

He turned to see Nash and Ethan hot on his heels in the Granite Fitness parking lot.

Shit. Maybe they'd come to make good on their promise to kick his ass for hurting Delaney. He unlocked his car, tossed his gym bag in the back, then turned to face the two men he'd learned to call friends, prepared to accept whatever they dished out.

"Haven't seen you around lately," Nash said.

*That's it?*

"I've been tied up with a business matter and the hiring of a new department chair." And avoiding the people who had come to matter most to him.

"We're having a bachelor party for Nash," Ethan added. "Low key, just a few friends, some juicy steaks, and a bottle of fifteen-year-old scotch I picked up for the occasion."

Devon nodded, but Nash and Ethan just looked at him. "What?"

"You in or not?" Nash prodded.

"Am I in?" Devon asked, confused.

"No, we're just telling you about the party, but you're not invited." Ethan laughed then sobered. "You know that, right? That you're invited?"

Devon scratched his chin. No. He didn't know that. "Aren't you two going to do something, kick my ass . . . something?"

"What for?" Nash's brows lifted in surprise.

"Delaney."

Ethan shouldered his gym bag. "You two are adults. I think you can work out your own problems without the two of us interfering."

"I became that guy—the one who broke Delaney's heart," Devon continued. Maybe he wanted his ass kicked. Maybe it would alleviate some of the guilt.

"So fix it." Nash folded his arms over his chest.

Devon scoffed. "Easier said than done."

Nash glanced at Ethan then back at Devon. "Let me ask you something." At Devon's nod, he continued, "You miss her?"

"Yes."

"You think about her all the time?"

"Yes."

"You want her back?"

"Yes."

"Then do yourself a favor. Let Delaney in. You won't find a more loving, accepting heart than hers. She doesn't know how *not* to love. Whether it's her friends, her flighty mother, or her students. It's in her DNA." Ethan smiled. "It's a rare trait."

A rare trait indeed. Something both of his parents lacked. But that didn't necessarily mean he lacked it as well, did it? Delaney had taught him that.

"Damn, man. That was beautiful," Nash said, staring at

Ethan like he'd just revealed the secrets of the universe. Then he slapped Devon on the back. "So, you in?"

"We aren't going to join hands and sing 'Kumbaya' or anything, are we?" Devon asked.

Ethan slapped him on the shoulder. "Nah. I thought we'd recite poetry instead."

Devon cracked a smile. "I'll be there."

Nash and Ethan headed for the gym.

"Oh, and Devon?" Nash called.

"Yes?"

"Groveling doesn't hurt."

THE NEXT DAY, Devon jumped into his car determined to find Delaney and convince her that Sam's love test was right.

His groveling plan had been delayed by some important business he needed to attend to. Business related to the bequest from his father. But everything was in place, and now he could face Delaney, on his knees if he had to, and beg her to take him back.

Heart in his throat, he pulled into Delaney's parking lot, ignoring the possibility that Delaney might say no.

DELANEY HAD GOTTEN HER WISH—HER Bachelor of Fine Arts in Romantic Fiction and Literature had been approved—but the victory now rang hollow.

Oh, she'd celebrated with Shelby and Sam at McGinty's. She'd received congratulations from Ethan and a few of her colleagues, but what she wanted more than anything was to thank Devon for his part in the committee's approval.

But she needed a plan. Which is where today's lunch-date-slash-strategy-session with her BFFs came into play. She'd just piled her hair on top of her head in a messy chic twist when her doorbell rang. She'd planned to meet Shelby and Sam at Ruby's, so unless they'd changed the plans, she couldn't imagine who was at her door.

Peering through the peephole, she blinked in confusion. Devon! And he looked a little rough around the edges, like he hadn't slept in days.

Well, join the club.

Taking a deep, cleansing breath, she opened the door, playing it cool, even though her insides were melting. "Hi."

"Hi." He stood, hands in the pockets of his khaki slacks, appearing awkward and unsure of himself. "Can I come in?"

She opened the door wider, indicating her acquiescence, and when he brushed past her, she closed her eyes and inhaled his scent, pressing a hand to her stomach where a hive of bees had taken up residence.

Closing the door, she faced him. "Can I get you something to drink?"

"No, thank you." His gaze held hers and her knees turned to Jell-O.

After several uncomfortable seconds, she cleared her throat. "How are you doing?"

"I've been better." He glanced down at the floor, a sad smile on his face.

"Yeah, I'm really sorry about your, um, Carter." She didn't know whether to refer to him as his father or not.

"Thanks, but that's not what I meant." He took a step toward her, and her heart took a hopeful leap inside her chest.

"No?" Her question came out in a breathy whisper.

He moved closer. "No." Closer still.

"Then what?"

He stood toe-to-toe with her, his gaze locked on hers. "I think you know."

She shook her head and realized she was crying when a tear spilled over onto her cheek.

He reached out his hand, capturing the tear with his thumb. "I've missed you." He cupped her face, and she closed her eyes as she leaned into his open palm. "I'm so sorry, Delaney. Can you ever forgive me?"

When she opened her eyes, she read the anguish on his face.

But–

She needed to know whether he could open his heart to her. To love. To let her see not just his strengths, but his weaknesses too.

She took his hand then let it fall by his side. "First, I need you to talk to me." Tapping his chest with her finger, she continued, "I need you to let me in. I need to know who you are, warts and all."

HE KNEW there would be a price to pay in winning Delaney back, and that price would be laying open his soul, revealing his shame. That he'd been unworthy of even his parents' love.

Delaney led him over to the sofa. She took a seat and faced him full on, so there would be no hiding. She listened intently, without interruption, while he laid it all out there. Every painful detail.

"When I was three years old, my mother left me with a man she claimed was my father, and I never heard from her again. That man, Carter Livingston, already the CEO of a

Fortune 500 company at age thirty-five, had little time or patience for me."

He stood, pacing her living room, unable to look her in the eye for fear of what he'd see—pity. Derision, even. "To his credit, though, he took responsibility for me, even if he never acknowledged his paternity."

"He hired a nanny until I was ready for kindergarten then shipped me off to boarding school for the entirety of my primary and secondary education. I, along with a few other kids, even remained on campus during the holiday and summer breaks, especially after Carter married and had three children. He provided my tuition and boarding at the school, gave me an allowance for clothing and other essentials, along with the occasional obligatory birthday gifts. Other than that, I never saw or heard from the man."

He finally looked across the room and into her face, expecting to see pity there, but instead, he saw understanding and acceptance.

"So, you see, I've never had a role model for love or relationships. In fact, when I signed up for Sam's research study, I was looking for a business partner, not a romantic one. A business partner kept me safe. A romantic one risked yet another rejection. And after being rejected by both my parents, I couldn't take another rejection. Especially from you."

"Oh, Devon."

She rose and came to him, pressing her lips to his in an achingly tender kiss, then gazed into his eyes. His soul. "It's his loss, you know. Your father missed out on a relationship with a smart, successful, compassionate man. Someone any father would be proud to call son."

He wrapped his arms around her, breathed her in. "Delaney, you make me want things I never thought were possible. Especially for me. And in the four months I've known you, you've taught me so much. But I have so much more to learn." He dropped his arms and took a step back. "I'm not sure I know what love is."

"It's a verb," she said, matter-of-fact.

He barked out a laugh. "I'm serious."

"So am I." She took his face in her hands and searched his eyes. "My mother always says love is something you do, not just something you feel."

He nodded then reached out for her hands. "I admire your determination and your persistence, and that you don't let adversity extinguish your love of life." He shook his head and smiled. "The cliché 'when life throws you lemons, make lemonade' was written for you." He gathered her close. "I love going to sleep with you at night and waking up next to you in the morning. If all those things are love it must mean . . . I love you, Delaney."

"I love you, Devon."

His heart swelled beyond its capacity. Content to just hold her, he closed his eyes, felt her heart beat. "Oh. I have something for you." Devon reached into his pocket and pulled out a folded, slightly crumpled piece of paper then handed it to her.

Brow furrowed, she took the paper then lifted her gaze to his face.

"Open it." He held his breath while Delaney read the letter, her expression going from curiosity to confusion to surprise.

"I don't–" She shook her head and her eyes flew to his. "You created a fund . . . for me?"

"For your degree program. That way you can afford to bring in the best in the business for your guest lectures, travel to the annual conference for romance writers, and the program will sustain for as long as you want it to."

"But, where–?"

"Did the money come from? Let's just say, I had a little help from . . . my father."

"So, he acknowledged you posthumously?" she asked, confused.

"No. Not exactly." He scratched his chin. "There was no remorseful note, no paternity test results. But I've decided it doesn't matter. I've never had a family. But you, Nash and Shelby, and Ethan and Sam are my family now."

"You're right about that. But you're wrong about something else. You know exactly what love is and how to give it."

"There's a saying in business—no risk, no reward. I guess the same thing applies to relationships."

"Yeah? And what else does that saying apply to?" She gazed up at him with so much tenderness, that the last of his armor fell away.

"Love?" He lifted his eyebrows.

"Good answer."

Placing his hands on her hips, he reeled her in. "By the way, I didn't support your proposal because I'm in love with you."

"And I didn't accept your apology because you supported my proposal."

"Good to know."

# EPILOGUE

The lovely old barn by the river was dressed for a summer afternoon wedding.

Delaney, a bridesmaid once again, had fulfilled her duties, and the afternoon reception was hers to enjoy.

Shelby made a beautiful bride, and Nash a handsome groom. As they recited their vows, Delaney had teared up. She always cried at weddings. Nothing new there. But mingled with the tears of happiness were tears of envy.

Two weddings in as many months. How much could a single woman take? Glancing down at her silk ice-blue sundress, she thought that it at least didn't look like a bridesmaid's dress.

She surveyed the barn, searching for Devon's dark brown hair among the guests. They'd only been officially dating for a month, but they'd been heading in that direction since the day they met four months earlier, albeit with a few detours and bumps in the road.

He was the most maddeningly stubborn, rigid, arrogant man she'd ever met. And she loved him unconditionally.

And he loved her. But would she ever walk down the aisle to see him standing at the other end waiting for her?

Patience was not her strongest virtue.

Sighing, she sipped from her glass of champagne as couples danced, laughed, and kissed. Where was he? He'd disappeared just when she wanted to dance. Likely on purpose.

She smiled when her gaze landed on Shelby and Nash, slowly swaying to an up-tempo song, like they were dancing to their own music, oblivious to everyone else around them.

It would soon be time to cut the cake and toss the bouquet. She'd caught so many bouquets in the last few years, and what had it gotten her? Nothing. This time, she refused to join the fray. Let someone else catch it. Maybe they would have better luck.

Hands grabbed her waist, startling her.

"Ever the bridesmaid, never the bride?" Devon spun her to face him, and she felt like throwing the champagne in his handsome face. "But what a beautiful bridesmaid you make." He kissed her on the lips. "Maybe that's the problem. Did you ever consider that? You're too beautiful a bridesmaid." He wore a mischievous grin. He loved to tease her, but today his jest hit bone.

Taking her glass from her hand, he set it on the table behind her and pulled her out onto the dance floor just as Etta James belted out the opening notes of "At Last."

She knew Devon wasn't fond of dancing, so the fact that he gathered her into his arms and began to sway touched her and made up for the unintentional jab. One arm around her waist, his other hand clasping her hand to his heart, he pressed his lips to her temple, reminiscent of the first time they'd danced. She sighed and leaned into him.

"Keep that up and we won't make it through this song

before I carry you off to a private corner for a make-out session."

"Promises, promises," she muttered against his neck.

She felt him smile against her hair. Closing her eyes, she lost herself in the feel of his arms around her, the length of him pressed to her. All too soon, the final notes of the song trailed off, and the DJ announced the cake-cutting.

Taking Devon's hand, they walked over to the linen-draped table displaying a confectionary creation almost too pretty to cut. Shelby and Nash did the honors then happily shoved cake into each other's faces, laughing like kids. Delaney rolled her eyes. Only Shelby wouldn't have minded have icing smeared all over her face on her wedding day.

The cake was sliced and served to the guests, then the DJ called for all the single ladies to step forward for the bouquet toss. Delaney planted her feet. Beyoncé's "Single Ladies" blared from the speakers.

"Aren't you going?" Devon asked, his brows lifted in question.

"No." She folded her arms across her chest.

"Isn't it a tradition?"

"Some traditions should be broken."

He gave her a little nudge. "Oh, go out there. Are you afraid you won't catch it?"

She turned and poked him in the chest. "For your information Dr. Mayfield, I've caught every bouquet thrown at me these last two years, and it's gotten me nowhere."

"Maybe this time is different," he said with a shrug.

"Come on ladies, don't be shy," the DJ encouraged. "Any other single ladies out there?"

"Yes!" Devon called. "This one." He pointed his finger at Delaney.

Mortified, she hissed at him. "Stop!"

He gave her a none-too-gentle push into the crowd of single ladies waiting for their chance to catch the bridal bouquet in the hopes of being the next to marry. Including the ancient widow, May Carpenter.

Delaney turned and gave him the evil eye, eliciting a laugh in response. God, she loved his laugh, all the more because it was so rare, but she'd heard more of it lately.

Shelby stood on the stage, grinned over her shoulder, then hurled the bouquet of blue hydrangeas and baby's breath over her shoulder.

Instinct kicked in and Delaney jumped for the bouquet as it sailed in her direction. Coming down with it, she tossed Devon a chagrined smile.

As Queen's "Another One Bites the Dust" opened, the DJ cajoled the single men in the crowd to step up for the garter toss. Amid whistles and catcalls, Shelby sat on a linen-covered chair, while Nash knelt in front of her and reached under her skirts for the garter. Shelby blushed then smacked his hand, as he'd obviously gotten fresh. Slipping the garter off her leg, he gave her a wink, and the females in the crowd audibly sighed.

Delaney looked around for Devon and was stunned to see him on the dance floor standing among the single men.

Nash turned his back on the crowd, pulled the garter back like a rubber band and launched it off the stage. Devon reached up and pulled the garter in like a fly ball in center-field. Delaney's mouth dropped open.

Amid pats on the back, Devon made his way to her. "You might want to close your mouth. I hear the flies can be murder around here in the summer."

Her jaw snapped shut.

"Come. I believe it's tradition for the single man who caught the garter—that would be me—to put it on the leg of the single woman who caught the bouquet—that would be you."

Speechless, she followed him up the steps to the stage and the waiting white linen-draped chair. Shelby and Nash stood hand-in-hand, big grins on their faces.

Delaney swallowed hard, scanned the crowd, all eyes on her. Ethan and Sam stood in front.

"Madam," Devon said, as he indicated for her to take a seat. Since her bridesmaid's dress was short, Devon didn't have to fumble beneath yards of fabric. He lifted her ankle and slowly, sensually, slid the blue lace garter up her leg, as the wedding guests shouted their encouragement. His warm hands glided up her bare legs, sending a frisson along her spine. Delaney's face burst into flames when his hands reached her thigh with a soft caress.

"While I'm down here–" Devon began, stirring up the audience even more with his innuendo.

Just as Delaney was about to smack his hand away, he reached into his pocket with his free hand and pulled out a little blue velvet box. Gasps arose from the crowd, and then they fell silent.

"Delaney, I realize we've only known each other four months, and most of that time was spent on opposite sides of an issue, but I can't think of another person I'd rather be on opposite sides of an issue with than you. Will you marry me?"

Barely able to see through the blur of her tears, she laughed, clutched his hand, and said, "Yes."

Sam's test had been right after all.

The guests applauded as Devon slid the beautiful

sapphire ring onto her finger. "Blue like your eyes," he whispered.

"It's perfect."

He took her hands and pulled her to him, kissing her lips. "Soon to be a bride instead of a bridesmaid."

# ABOUT THE AUTHOR

Rebecca Heflin is an award-winning author who has dreamed of writing romantic fiction since she was fifteen and her older sister sneaked a copy of Kathleen Woodiwiss' Shanna to her and told her to read it.

Never quite sure what she wanted to be when she grew up, Rebecca didn't attend college until age 30, and earned her bachelor's in literature, before going on to complete her law degree.

Ever the late bloomer, Rebecca finally turned her attention to fulfilling her dream of writing, and published her first novel at age 48. When not passionately pursuing her dream, Rebecca is busy with her day-job at a major state university.

She and her husband are also co-founders of a non-profit organization, which raises money to help cancer patients and their families.

Rebecca's pen name is an abbreviated version of her great-great grandmother's name: Sarah Anne Rebecca Heflin Apple Smith. Whew! And you wonder why she shortened it.

Rebecca writes women's fiction and contemporary romance, and she is a member of Romance Writers of America (RWA), Florida Romance Writers, RWA Contemporary Romance, and Florida Writers Association. Rebecca and her mountain-climbing husband live in central Virginia.

Sign up for Rebecca's newsletter for all the latest news on upcoming releases, appearances, and contests.

www.rebeccaheflin.com
rebecca@rebeccaheflin.com

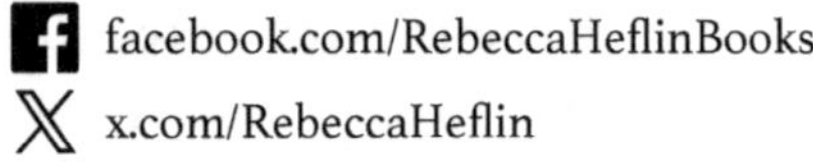

facebook.com/RebeccaHeflinBooks

x.com/RebeccaHeflin

# ALSO BY REBECCA HEFLIN

*THE PROMISE OF CHANGE*

*RESCUING LACEY*

**DREAMS COME TRUE SERIES**

*DREAMS OF PERFECTION, BOOK 1*

*SHIP OF DREAMS, BOOK 2*

*DREAMS OF HER OWN, BOOK 3*

***STERLING UNIVERSITY SERIES***

*ROMANCING DR. LOVE, BOOK 1*

*WINNING DR. WENTWORTH, BOOK 2*

***SEASONS OF NORTHRIDGE SERIES***

*A SEASON TO DANCE, BOOK 1*

*A SEASON TO LOVE, BOOK 2*

*A SEASON TO REMEMBER, BOOK 3*

*A SEASON TO GIVE, BOOK 4*

**WHIRLWIND ROMANCE**

UNDER THE PARIS MOON